KEEP
HER
SAFE

D0999158

ALSO BY RICHARD PARKER

Follow You
Hide and Seek
Scare Me
Stop Me
Stalk Me

KEEP HER SAFE

RICHARD PARKER

Bookouture

Published by Bookouture in 2018

An imprint of StoryFire Ltd.
Carmelite House
50 Victoria Embankment
London EC4Y 0DZ

www.bookouture.com

ISBN: 978-1-78681-312-1
eBook ISBN: 978-1-78681-311-4

To my big brother Chris – thanks for all you do for me – and sister-in-law, Alison, for always spreading the word about my books!

CHAPTER ONE

Maggie couldn't work out what sort of noise had woken her. As the shadowy ceiling of her bedroom came into focus she turned to her clock and squinted: 10:13 p.m. Her lack of sleep that week had prompted her to go to bed early, but she'd been there less than an hour. She waited for whichever sound had chiselled into her dreams, breath paused in her chest.

Nothing. Just the vague patter of snow on the window-pane. The latest storm had started in earnest around six in the evening.

Maggie lived in the first house on a narrow, dead-end row, and now she listened for footsteps outside her window. Nothing. *Maybe it had come from next door?* Mrs Serafina was in her eighties and often had her TV up loud. She couldn't hear it. Maggie still didn't breathe out.

Maggie lived in Whitsun, a small New England town. Most of her neighbours in Bozeman Street were retired so noise at night was minimal. *Could it have been Chuck Bretton's dog?* It rarely barked though.

A thud from downstairs. Maggie immediately sat up, blood draining from where it had been throbbing in her eardrums. *Had that actually been inside the house?* She always bolted the inner kitchen door before coming up to bed, so if anyone had broken in through the back one they'd have had to deal with a second before being able to access the lounge and the rest of the house.

The front door of her red-brick Georgian row house was solid oak and had two deadbolts. The window of the lounge was triple glazed. If someone were to get in, the rear would be the most likely place as it backed onto the edge of a forest.

Maggie waited and felt her chest tightening as her lungs strained for oxygen. She'd done this to herself the past few nights. Scared herself into believing that someone was inside her home.

Thud.

Maggie swung her legs out of bed and placed her bare feet on the cold carpet. Penny, her baby daughter, hadn't woken. She was a great sleeper. Everyone at the mothers' group couldn't believe how long she stayed down. At thirty-four, Maggie was one of the oldest there, and the others looked to her for support, like she wasn't winging motherhood as much as they were. Penny's exemplary sleeping patterns convinced everyone it was down to Maggie's parenting skills. But Penny was eighteen months and, despite Maggie's best efforts, still hadn't taken a step or spoken her first word.

Thud.

Was it the loose guttering getting blown against the side of the house as it had been last night? But she'd fixed that and tonight there was no wind. She breathed in the cool air of the room and quickly slid her white robe over her powder blue pyjamas. *Where were her slippers? No time to locate them.* She clenched herself and quietly twisted the handle of the wooden door.

It had expanded in the frame with the damp, and she had to give it an almighty tug to free it. The nursery door was straight ahead and exactly nine paces away. She'd counted her steps there so many times now. Maggie found the switch for the landing light to her left, turned it on and waited.

The bulb buzzed above her.

If only her mothers' group could see her now. *How many times had she done this over the past few nights: loitered on the landing like a frightened kid, looking over the banister to the stairs below and preparing to lock herself in with Penny?*

Snow rustled on the darkened skylight, but she couldn't discern anything else. She took a pace forward and looked over the banister. She could see the kitchen door was still locked below.

Maggie waited, her heart feeling as if it was frantically clawing its way up her chest. She still didn't move. Her thoughts were rewinding to the previous week, when she'd been sick with terror outside another door…

The long window on the landing was black. But even though she knew it looked across to nothing but the tree-lined horizon, she couldn't help but think that somebody was watching her standing frozen there.

In the absence of any more sounds, Maggie pushed open the nursery door. As she entered the dark room and switched on the light, there was a noise inside – much louder than any Penny could have been making from her crib: a sliding hiss that drew Maggie's attention to the window.

Somebody was coming through it.

CHAPTER TWO

The figure was halfway through, their bulk bent over the ledge and partially concealed by the curtains their body was bulging out. *Were they wearing a cloak?*

Maggie lunged for Penny. She scooped her out of her crib and clasped her tight as the figure's weight landed on the carpet and shuddered the floorboards. As they stood, the hood of their dark blue poncho glistened from the rain.

Maggie yelled then. An incoherent warning that came from deep inside her. She hoped it would briefly startle them.

The figure froze, and Maggie saw blue surgical gloves clutching a carving knife. Her shoulder butted hard into the doorframe as she reversed from the nursery.

Get back to the bedroom. Lock the door, she thought.

Fingers seized her bob of dark hair. Maggie twisted her head, clutched Penny to her chest and crouched as she made for her open bedroom door.

But the hand was yanking her back.

Maggie could feel and hear the roots of her hair rip. She jerked her body sideways to escape and slammed into the banister slats.

She was on one knee, the carpet burning it as her attacker lurched with her. Their wet bulk was on her back, but the grip hadn't loosened. Maggie cradled Penny with one arm and turned awkwardly to hit out at the face behind her.

Her fist connected with their throat, and she caught a glimpse of the features within the hood as they reacted to the pain. Maggie whipped her head away from the rubber fingers, grabbed one of the banister slats and used it to heave herself to her feet. She could see the knife on the carpet to the right of her but knocked it with her foot to the left. It slid through the banister and dropped down the stairs.

A hand grasped her ankle and tugged her back. She wrapped her arms around Penny as she fell and tried not to crush her.

'Get off me!' Rage crowded out her fear as she turned and kicked back at the figure with her free foot. Maggie's bare sole connected with an arm reaching out to her.

Maggie kicked again, and this time caught their chin. As they grunted, she wrenched her ankle from their grip and slid away on her behind. She held Penny tight to her chest.

But they pounced at her again, crawling forward on all fours to intercept her before she could enter the bedroom. A hand tried to secure her leg once more, and Maggie kicked at it as she slammed her back against the wall beside the door.

Maggie turned and jammed her free elbow back as the figure tried to stop her getting inside. She heard the breath pushed out of them, smelt their sourness as she stood, grappled with the edge of the door and attempted to shut it.

The figure was blocking it, and Maggie pushed harder. But her weight was squashing Penny. If she repositioned herself, however, it would be the tiny release of pressure they needed to get in.

Maggie could hear Penny snuffling and starting to cry against her breast. Her bare feet slid on the carpet as the figure drove their weight against the panel.

'You're not coming in here!' Maggie snarled through bared teeth and pedalled with her feet, trying to concentrate all of her energy into the shoulder blade that was above Penny.

Her attacker puffed air as they rammed themselves repeatedly against the wood.

Maggie waited for the gap between the blows to the door and turned swiftly, bashing her spine against it and digging her heels in. She now had Penny in a safer position.

Maggie could see her cell phone on the nightstand. It was only about four feet away, but there was no way she could pick it up. The figure threw itself at the door, and the impact juddered her chest and lifted her from the panel before she lodged herself in place again.

She leaned back harder and felt the door slide half into the frame. But the expanded wood wouldn't close flush. The door cracked with another blow, and Maggie prepared for their next run up. She battered the side of her body against the door, crying out as it banged shut. Maggie quickly turned the key in the lock.

Their fists were against the panel now, banging repeatedly with frustration and almost splitting the wood.

Maggie backed away, unsure how long it would hold.

'Ssshhh, ssshhh.' Maggie tried to placate Penny, but her daughter's mouth had widened, and the dry scrape of tears had turned into a howl.

The noise at the door didn't abate.

Maggie sat on the edge of her bed with Penny and regarded her cell again. There was definitely no way she would use it.

She'd seen the face of her attacker and, even though Maggie hadn't recognised it, knew she couldn't call the police on her.

'Ssshhh, ssshhh.'

CHAPTER THREE

A fissure appeared in the bottom panel of the door. The woman was kicking it as well as beating it.

'I've called the cops!' Maggie shouted over Penny's bawling.

The noise stopped.

'Better start running!' Maggie tried to calm her daughter so she could listen for the intruder's exit. 'Ssshhh. That's enough of that now.' But she didn't hear footsteps retreating to the nursery. 'Ssshhh.' She stood from the bed but didn't move too far back to the door.

Penny's body wriggled in her arms as Maggie strained to hear. The torn roots of her hair pulsed in time with the scraped skin of her knee. 'Ssshhh.' She rocked Penny, and her daughter's sobs became less frequent. Maggie's circulation refused to slow, and she couldn't hear anything above it.

The door shook in its frame and Penny's yelling intensified. It sounded like her female intruder was using something solid to try and bash the door in.

'You're not going to get in here!' But she really wasn't sure. 'Not in time. Go now. You can still escape before they arrive.' Maggie looked at her phone for the third time but knew that was all she was going to do with it.

The wood thundered again.

'I know why you've come here!' Maggie shouted over Penny.

Another strike to the door opened a crack all the way up it. Many more and the whole thing would break apart.

'And exactly why you can't leave until I'm dead.'

The assault halted.

Maggie stroked Penny's head but it didn't soothe her. 'You're a mother like me, aren't you?'

No response from the landing.

'I know you're terrified right now. Speak to me.' As Penny's full-throated wailing continued, Maggie could see a shadow flit across the split.

'Open this door!' a frazzled female voice demanded from the other side of it.

She sounded young to Maggie. 'You've been given my name.' Maggie gently jiggled Penny. 'Haven't you?'

'Yes,' the voice eventually conceded. 'You're Maggie Walsh.'

Maggie closed her eyes. Now there was no doubt.

'Is this part of the test?'

'No.' Maggie slowly slid open the drawer of the nightstand.

'Then how do you know? You must be part of it.'

'No. I just know what you've been asked to do.'

'How?' Hysteria had crept into the woman's voice.

'Somebody has taken your baby, haven't they?' There was no reply but then Maggie heard the woman sniff. 'And they told you to come here and stab me otherwise your child won't be returned.'

'Yes.' The female intruder eventually answered. 'Tell me how you know.' Her voice trembled.

'Because four days ago I was told to do the same.' Maggie took out what she kept in the drawer. It was Jeff's .38 snubbie revolver and she'd fully loaded it.

CHAPTER FOUR

'What's your name?' Maggie pointed the weapon directly at the door. She'd fired guns on a range before, but not this one.

'Tell me it ends here. That this has been a sick joke and you're going to give Abigail back to me.'

Maggie shivered. She recognised the raw desperation in her voice. She hugged Penny tighter and hated what she was about to say. 'No. I can't help you find your daughter. I wish someone could have done the same for me.'

'She's only twenty-one months,' the woman's voice quavered.

Maggie bounced Penny. Her eyelids were getting heavy. The crying was wearing her out. 'I'm sorry. I can't help you. You have to leave now.'

'He said if I don't go through with this I'll never see her again.'

Maggie shut her eyes. 'Go back to him. Say you'll do anything.' But she'd tried the same. She'd begged but been told there was only one course of action that would return Penny to her.

'He's not going to listen. If I let you live…' She couldn't finish the rest of the sentence.

Maggie nodded but kept the barrel steady. 'What's your name?'

'I'm not doing this,' the other woman replied warily.

'Doing what?'

'Letting you use my name so you can reason with me.'

Maggie stiffened. That wasn't the response of someone who was about to fall apart. But if she was like Maggie she'd probably spent hours keying herself up to do it. 'Just take a breath.' Now

Penny's sobs were slowing, Maggie could hear the woman's dry panting near the door.

'Why should I listen to anything you say? I don't know you. I was only given this address today.'

'But you know I'm a mother living on her own. How old are you?'

'Quiet, let me think.'

'My child, Penny, she's eighteen months.'

'I don't want to know.'

She didn't want to know who Maggie was or who was about to become an orphan. But she had to dissuade her, because the only other alternative was gripped cold in her fist. 'I don't know who you are but, like me, you have to be sickened by what you've been told to do.'

The shadow moved past the crack in the door again.

'Even if Abigail's life depends on it.'

'Don't use her name either.' She was breathing faster now.

Was she psyching herself up? 'You told me her name. She means everything to you, right?'

'Stop talking.'

'So does my Penny. And if you think I'm about to let you deprive her of her only parent then you'd better think very carefully before coming near this door again.' But this was what she shouldn't be doing. If she became aggressive, if she gave this woman even half a reason to want to return it, it made the job she'd been given that much more bearable. 'I know you'll do anything for her.' She softened her voice. 'But believe me, I'm prepared to do the same. A second time.'

CHAPTER FIVE

'OK,' the voice on the landing said eventually.

What the hell did that mean? 'OK, you're leaving?'

There was a pause. 'No. OK, I'm prepared to believe this happened to you.'

But Maggie wasn't buying it. 'Why?'

'Because time is running out and I don't have a choice.'

Or was she biding time until she could take her by surprise?

'I need to know one thing though.'

'What?' Maggie could see the shadow of her intruder's feet at the gap under the door.

'Have you really called the cops?' Her voice suddenly sounded small, like a child's.

Maggie considered how to reply. *What would be the most convincing answer?* If she said she had, would that mean her intruder would attack in the small amount of time she thought she had before they arrived? If the woman were to believe that Maggie had done the same as she'd been told to do when her child had been threatened, 'no' would be more convincing. Maggie shouldn't *want* to summon the cops, particularly if they arrested her intruder. If she revealed why she was there they'd then question Maggie about her own mission.

With no alibi for that night, the police could easily find out what she'd done, and Maggie couldn't countenance the notion of them taking Penny away. She looked down at her daughter dozing in her arms. 'It doesn't matter,' she called. 'I'm not leaving this room until you're gone of your own accord or in a pair of handcuffs.'

'If you won't tell me, maybe I'll take my chances. But if your story's true, you wouldn't have called them. If they arrest me, I'll tell them you've just admitted to doing the same as I have.'

The threat to her and Penny was escalating. This woman was smart.

'Did you call them?'

'No.' Maggie swallowed and waited.

An exhalation and then silence.

What was going through her mind now? 'That's the honest answer. I can also tell you that it doesn't matter one way or the other because I'm holding a loaded gun.'

The shadow moved swiftly sideways.

'It belonged to my ex but I know how to use it. I'm not a great shot but from this distance I'm not going to miss you coming through the door.' She tried to control the tremor in her voice. 'I don't want to fire it in front of Penny, but I will if I have to.'

The other woman absorbed this for a few moments. 'You just told me you called the police when you didn't. Why should I believe you've got a gun in there?'

'You can find out if you go near that door again.'

'I've only got until sunrise. Give me a straight answer.'

'So you can do a risk assessment? Decide whether it's safe to force your way in?'

'Fire a shot.'

'I've told you. Not with Penny in here.'

'Then I have no proof your gun exists. The room you're in is at the far corner of your house. You won't be able to bang on the wall to attract your neighbour, and the window only overlooks the forest.'

She must have been watching Maggie's home as Maggie had *her* target's; waiting and trembling while she came to the same conclusion she had. That she should bide her time until after the bedroom light had been switched off. 'Did you bring anything else? Other than the knife?'

The floorboard creaked under the woman's weight. And Maggie hoped she wouldn't play dumb.

'Just a knife from the block at home.'

'You got a phone with you?'

'Yes,' the woman said suspiciously.

'You on WhatsApp?'

'Yeah.'

'OK, give me your number. I'll WhatsApp you a photo of me with the gun in my hand.'

Silence.

'Come on.' Maggie felt emboldened. 'That's going to be the quickest way of settling this. I'll send you a photo of my gun.'

'My cell is in the car,' she eventually responded.

'Convenient. Isn't he in touch with you on that?'

'Yes.'

'He was with me too. Told me to silence the ringer when I went inside the house. I'm surprised he didn't do the same with you.'

'I said, it's in the car,' she replied, tersely.

'Are you parked nearby?'

'How stupid d'you think I am? I'm not fetching it.'

'Why not? I've told you I haven't called the police.'

'Yes, that's what you *told* me. But even if you haven't you can still escape while I'm gone.'

'Escape where?'

'Even if you didn't want to involve your neighbours there's a huge forest for you to hide in back there.'

'OK, that was a dumb thing for me to say. Listen, I don't believe your cell is in your car, so why don't I send you the image like I said?'

'It's in the car,' the woman snapped, barely holding her temper in check.

'OK. Then you're just going to have to believe I've got this gun in my hand.' Maggie gripped it harder almost as if she had to convince herself. 'And I'll have to believe you just have that carving knife.'

CHAPTER SIX

Holly took her iPhone from her back jeans pocket and looked at the display.

10:27 p.m.

She had until sunrise. That was just before seven. Eight and a half hours, and Maggie Walsh was now locked away, out of her reach. Her rubber-clad hand shook as she checked to see if there were any other text messages for her to open. Nothing.

Her throat ached from Maggie's blow and adrenaline rushed through her, but she could feel the beginnings of hesitancy taking hold and couldn't allow that. Maggie had to be dead when she left the house. It was her or Abigail. If a child had to be orphaned, it would be Maggie's. Holly couldn't leave Abigail in the hands of that man for one second longer than she had to.

She'd tucked herself against the banister in case Maggie tried to shoot her through the door. The snow clumped against the skylight above. *Where had her carving knife gone?* She peered over the darkened stairs but couldn't see a sign of it.

'So how close did you get to calling the police?' the voice from the bedroom asked.

Holly knew Maggie was playing for time. Trying to engage her and talk her out of what she had to do.

'Bet you he's told you what would happen to Abigail if you did that…'

Holly's stomach shrank every time she thought about what he'd said in his text message. *No cops. Abigail's life depends on that.*

Holly hadn't considered involving the police since she'd received it. 'Speak to me.'

'Shut up!' Holly put the phone away and tugged down her hood. Her curly, auburn hair was tucked inside a black wool watch cap, and her head was sweltering hot. She couldn't remove it though. Didn't want to leave any strands inside the house. She'd bought all her clothes with cash from an army surplus place outside of town. The jeans, the boots, the black pullover and waterproof navy poncho, Holly was going to burn them all as soon as she was done, just like she'd been instructed.

There was no choice. If she wanted to see Abigail again she had to do the unthinkable.

'I picked up the phone to the police. Must have been four times I nearly dialled the number. But neither of us can do that...'

Holly had to ignore her voice. Whatever Maggie said to her would be in the interests of protecting her own child.

'I know you're probably more scared than I am right now...'

Holly was petrified. Briefly, she'd thought that Maggie had been part of some obscene prank. That Holly was being tested and that Abigail would be returned as soon as she'd proved her intent to carry out murder. But even though Holly clearly wasn't about to be released from what she'd undertaken, Maggie Walsh had given her a glimmer of hope. If she was telling the truth, she'd done the same. Been threatened and manipulated by the man at the end of the phone. And she'd had her child returned to her.

'Yes. I am scared,' Holly answered her. 'Weren't you?' She had to know how it was possible for Maggie to have done something like this. She waited for her response. Eager to hear it, even though she had to dismiss everything she said.

'I was paralysed. It was like I waited outside and watched myself walk to the back door. I don't even remember breaking the glass. I tried to bypass my emotions. Tried to forget my family and friends and not think about how they would perceive what I was doing.'

Holly closed her eyes and shook her head. 'Even though that's what you're trying to make *me* do.'

Penny grumbled behind the panel.

'She's getting hungry,' Maggie informed her. 'I'm going to have to breastfeed her.'

Holly felt her maternal instincts trickling through the intensity of the moment. She fought against them.

'I can still do it and hold the gun on the door.'

Holly was sure it was part of Maggie's strategy. She had to repel the image of her breastfeeding Penny. If she delayed much longer she could never bring herself to do it. And that meant she'd never be able to breastfeed Abigail again.

'Just wait.' Maggie seemed to sense Holly's thought process.

Holly pulled out a Browning Buck Mark Camper handgun and pointed it firmly at the door handle.

'Hear me out.'

Holly's father had always owned guns and taught her how to squeeze the trigger when she was fourteen, but she had no experience of the weapon she'd bought less than twenty-four hours before she'd broken into Maggie's house. She'd decided to bring it along as backup. *Was it really possible to shoot off the lock?* That was something she'd only seen in movies. *Would the bullet ricochet around the landing and kill her?* And she didn't want to endanger Penny.

Perhaps her only way in through the door was to repeatedly kick it down. But then Maggie might shoot her through the wood. That's if she actually had a gun. After her offer to send her an image, however, she guessed she did. *Or did she know that Holly would never agree to trade numbers?*

'There is another way out of this.'

Of course she'd tell her that.

'I found it.'

Holly could boot once and hard under the handle, use the bathroom as cover and see if Maggie pulled the trigger.

'I didn't go through with it… I didn't murder anyone.'

CHAPTER SEVEN

Holly's gun arm remained rigid. 'You're lying. Are you telling me you refused to murder someone but you still got Penny back?' But every cell of her wanted to believe that.

'Not exactly.' Maggie sounded evasive.

'Then what?'

Penny started crying.

'Wait.'

Holly attempted to block the sound out. 'Answer me.'

Maggie did, but her words were incoherent.

'Say again.'

'Things didn't go to plan.'

Even though Maggie's voice was much lower than before, Holly could just about understand her. She was about to step to the door but stopped herself. *Was it a ploy to get her closer so Maggie could take a shot?* 'Speak up.'

'I'm being quiet for her sake.'

'Not tonight. You have a child. I don't.'

'I'm sorry.' The apology was earnest.

Maggie was an older mother. Holly was barely twenty-three – still felt like a child herself sometimes. And now she had to make *this* choice. Her midwife had told her young parents were the best because they didn't question what they had to do. Holly had thought she was insane. 'Tell me what happened.' She tried not to picture Maggie on the bed cradling Penny.

'I watched the house. I'd been told the girl who rented the place lived alone.'

Holly had been told the same.

'After he told me what he was going to do to Penny…'

Holly waited. Knew Maggie was looking into her daughter's face.

'I threw up when I got out of the car.'

She wanted to hear every detail of the same stark dread she'd experienced earlier this evening, but Holly knew that would take time she didn't have. 'Just tell me what happened.' Her phone buzzed in her back pocket.

'I got inside no problem.'

Holly took out her iPhone. There was a text message. She tapped the icon with her rubber-clad thumb. It was from him. He called himself *Babysitter*:

?

He wanted a progress report. *Was he watching?* She'd been looking for signs of him all day; if he was, he knew how to keep himself concealed. Holly looked at the blank pane of the long window of the landing and caught her own reflection there; standing with the gun extended from her poncho, the face above it that of someone she'd never seen before.

'It was when I got into the house that it went wrong.'

CHAPTER EIGHT

From the kitchen Maggie could see the weak light from the landing dimly illuminating the staircase through the glass panel of the lounge door. Her lips were sealed shut and breath whistled softly through her nostrils. The smells of the house were vivid – stale cooking and overpowering sandalwood air freshener – so potent she thought she might vomit again.

The house wasn't in a very good neighbourhood, and she'd had to wait for kids playing on the waste ground around it to disperse before she could position herself at the back fence of the tiny yard.

Her black, slip-on canvas shoes came to a halt on the lounge carpet. Behind her the refrigerator suddenly kick-started and rattled whatever china was on top of it. The noise seemed deafening, and she almost turned around and strode back out the rear door she'd just entered.

Somebody moved across the top of the landing, their shadow briefly flitting over and darkening the bottom of the stairs. Maggie's heart stalled. Janet Braun was up. Even though Maggie had seen the light go out just after midnight and had waited over two hours, the girl was awake. *Was it because she'd heard Maggie break the glass of the back door?*

She waited, rigid, anticipating her coming down the stairs or the sound of her calling the police. But she couldn't hear a panicked voice on the phone.

A flush hissed.

The shadow briefly blocked the light from the landing again, and Maggie discerned a door softly close shut. She took a breath.

But now Janet would be awake. If she'd given in to the temptation of entering earlier, she probably would have been in a deeper sleep. It was how Maggie wanted to find her – oblivious to her presence so she could push the knife into her chest and cover her mouth at the same time.

Should she wait now? Give her an hour before going up there? Maggie could just make out the top edge of the couch from the light spilling in from upstairs. She headed for it and flinched silently as her shin struck the hard edge of the coffee table.

She paused, listening for signs of movement overhead and then slowly lowered herself onto the couch. It was leather and creaked as it gradually took her weight. Maggie eventually settled herself but didn't lean back. She unzipped her Parka to allow some air to her neck but kept her baseball cap on. Babysitter had advised her to wear headgear so no stray hairs escaped.

Her phone vibrated in her pocket, and she immediately took it out. It was him:

?

She responded:

Have you fed Penny?

She's asleep on my chest.

Maggie trembled with hatred. The notion of Penny's face lying against the warmth of him, that her daughter's tiny ear could probably hear the heartbeat of that monster, filled her with repulsion. Better she was rested there than he'd done anything to her though. That he'd harmed her in the ways he'd threatened. Or maybe she wasn't. Perhaps he was just tormenting her.

Sunrise.

Was his one word of encouragement.

That was just before seven. Five hours to find the courage to go upstairs and push a knife into a complete stranger. *Who was the woman in the bedroom and, if Babysitter was so capable of inflicting the violence he'd promised for Penny, why didn't he kill Janet Braun himself?*

Her eyes were becoming accustomed to the darkness now and she took in the black TV screen hanging on the wall in front of her and the few shelves of indistinguishable ornaments either side of it. Then she saw the pram, and her stomach slid down inside her. Janet Braun was a mother too.

She rose so slowly from the couch that it didn't make a sound. Then she carefully crossed the room, avoiding the coffee table so she could double-check. The pram juddered as her foot gently bumped it, and its tiny toys filled with beads rattled where they hung across the seat.

She asked herself why this would alter anything. She'd been prepared to stab another human being to save her child, someone who would be mourned by her family and friends. But it did make a significant difference to Maggie, and the concept of another defenceless child being put in jeopardy because of her actions revolted her.

How old was the child? Nausea rolled hard over her. But it wasn't physical; this resonated through who she was. Something she'd been trying to forget, at least for the time she was inside the house. But Maggie knew that would be impossible now she had so much time to wait while Janet Braun fell asleep again.

She put her hand against the wall to steady herself. She was wearing clear surgical gloves. Babysitter had told her to buy them.

She'd asked him who Janet Braun was. Babysitter had replied: 'The key to Penny's cage.'

He'd told her something else about Janet. Something repellent. It was probably a lie to make her carry out his orders but that's what she had to focus on now: Penny's safety. Not the pram in front of her or the child who would lie inside it. They would be taken care of. When Maggie left their mother dead the child would still be safe, safer than Penny was right now, and young enough to sustain the shock of a mother's removal. But Maggie's rationalisation disgusted her. *How would she live with this, even if Babysitter did give Penny back?*

The truth of that was like a hook dragging through her. There was no guarantee that Penny would be returned. And the image that Babysitter had sent her was no assurance she was still alive.

The room spun, and Maggie gripped the edge of the pram with her other hand. *What would Janet Braun do? If presented with the same stark choice, what course of action would she take?* There was only one for any mother. Maggie asked herself which person she would rather be: the mother sleeping above or the one aware of what was about to happen.

Her insides roiled, and she felt as if she might suffocate if she didn't immediately climb the stairs with the blade in her hand. But it had only been a matter of minutes since Janet had returned to bed and chances were she was still awake.

Maggie wondered if the baby slept in a crib in the bedroom with her. If Janet woke and screamed while Maggie stabbed her… She couldn't have an infant present at the murder of their mother.

She pulled both her hands against her chest and clenched them tight. She had to rein in her panic. Breathing in through her nose she cracked her lips to release it and then took out her iPhone. She sent Babysitter a message.

Am in house. Janet Braun has a baby.

His reply was swift.

I know. Aren't you grateful I'm not asking you to kill the child too?

Maggie typed a response.

Please, please don't make me do this.

Sunrise.

Maggie barely restrained a sob from escaping.

CHAPTER NINE

Maggie closed her eyes and kept them tightly shut. The blood roared through her ears, and she desperately wanted to dive into the patterns in front of her eyelids and never emerge. She counted the seconds of minute after minute, not moving, her body solid and feeling as if it were suspended from the heavy hook still scoring her insides.

She let the room back in thirty minutes later, knew she couldn't physically wait any longer. There had been no sound from upstairs since Janet had returned to the bedroom. If she had a baby, there was every chance it might start crying and then she would have to count all over again.

She turned from the pram and walked stiffly to the door. As she put her palm on the handle the rubber of her glove squeaked. Maggie slowly depressed it and the lock softly clicked out of the frame. She allowed it to swing to her before gently pulling it open.

The hallway smelt more like cooking than the kitchen. The aroma was good, like cookies, like home. It couldn't have been further removed from what she was about to do.

The landing light illuminated all the flecks of dirt and fluff on the oatmeal stair carpet. Maggie crossed the worn blue hallway rug and put her foot on the first step. She shifted her weight onto it and waited for the wood to groan underneath her. It was silent. Lightly grabbing the handrail she painstakingly climbed, resisting the temptation to accelerate and testing each stair before continuing.

The seventh had a loose board. It began to creak as she pressed on it with her right foot, so she gripped the rail harder and stepped over it, stretching her leg to assess the next. That one was fine, so she dragged herself up. But the action put all her weight on her toes, and the wood cracked loudly.

Maggie stayed stock still, listening for movement above. She didn't budge for a few minutes, even after she was sure she hadn't woken Janet. Only four stairs left. It took her another minute to ascend those, and she tentatively probed the landing before she settled both her feet there.

To her right was the bathroom door, slightly ajar. To her immediate left was what she assumed was the sealed one to Janet's bedroom. Before that was a door with one word written on it.

DANIEL

It was written in the eyes of a row of frogs sitting along a lily pad. Maggie tried to avert her gaze as she turned towards Janet's bedroom and put her hand on the knife handle in her jacket pocket. But as she reached it she knew she wouldn't be able to stop herself from looking inside the nursery.

She listened at Janet's door and heard a very definite sound of snoring coming from within. *Just peek in Daniel's room for a couple of seconds…*

Why was she doing this? How could this make the task she had any easier? But Maggie needed to see Janet's child. Not out of curiosity, but because she wanted to remind herself of what she was sacrificing of her own if she didn't do what Babysitter told her to do.

She put her fingers on the panel and softly pushed. The aroma from inside had already reached her. But here it was undiluted; the smell of the sleeping baby triggering a reaction in her she hoped would act as a catalyst. The atmosphere in the nursery was like a vicarious shot, an intoxicating hit that sparked a procession of intense emotions.

Where was Penny sleeping now? How could she possibly allow her to be in danger for a second longer than she needed to be?

Maggie could see the crib in the nightlight that projected tiny stars and constellations onto the wall and ceiling. Daniel was breathing shallowly on his side, turned away from her. She didn't want to see his face. Just needed to make sure he was fast asleep. She could call the police anonymously from a payphone afterwards. Say she'd heard a disturbance. That way they'd find Daniel. Probably before he'd even woken up.

She pulled herself out of the room and leaned against the wall outside, breathing in the cooler air there. Maggie wanted to wake now. She'd had countless nightmares when she'd done something unspeakable, and the relief she'd experienced when she'd opened her eyes was like that bad chunk of her suddenly evaporating. That wasn't going to happen now.

But she repeated what she'd said to herself since she'd been waiting in the car outside. This wasn't about her. This was only about Penny. She was an instrument of her freedom.

The key to Penny's cage.

Maggie slid the carving knife out of her pocket. It was Babysitter's stipulation.

The acid rose in her throat as she felt its weight in her clenched fist. 'Pull the door, walk quickly into the room, cover Janet's mouth and push the blade up under the ribcage.' That's how Babysitter had told her to do it. 'Jab the blade there three or four times to make sure you cut through the muscle.'

Maggie slowly filled her lungs, kept the air hissing in until she imagined them solid inside her. She was gripping the knife so tight the tops of her right fingers had started to go numb. Maggie tensed her calves in readiness.

Above the clamour of her circulation, she noticed the snoring had ceased. Momentarily, she hung back straining for sounds that

Janet was still asleep. But Maggie couldn't delay any longer. She had to go now or she knew her conscience would prevent her.

Pressing the handle all the way she swung her arm in with the door, took three paces through it and turned to the bed. The duvet was gathered in the middle of the mattress and nightlights were switched on at both sides. Maggie squinted against them and tried to make out what position Janet was in.

She could discern a shape under the quilt and quickly estimated the situation. There were two people in the bed; she could see four legs entwined.

Maggie didn't dare to blink but stood transfixed, waiting for one of them to wake and sit up.

One of their shallow breaths faltered, and Maggie considered darting back to the door. But neither of the naked forms moved. Maggie had watched the house for hours. She'd only seen Janet come home mid-afternoon. The man had already been there.

There was no way she could continue now. She couldn't be expected to kill both of them. If she stabbed one surely the other would attack. She lingered there for a few seconds longer, watching the duvet constantly rising and falling with their combined, out-of-sync breaths.

Maggie slid the knife swiftly back into the pocket of her Parka and crept from the room. She gritted her teeth, ready for a commotion behind her as they registered her presence, but none came.

She pulled the door shut quietly behind her and made her way back down the stairs, carefully treading on the parts she'd memorised when she'd ascended them. When she was in the hallway Maggie knew there was nothing more she could do but that she couldn't just walk out of the house. She stepped into the darkened lounge, delicately closed the glass door and messaged Babysitter.

There are two people asleep in the bedroom.

Maggie girded herself in readiness for his command to head back upstairs.

She looked at the clock of her cell: 2:49 a.m. Plenty of hours until sunrise.

He made her wait until 2:52 before he answered.

That will get very messy. Get yourself out of there, Maggie. Quickly.

CHAPTER TEN

'And he still gave you Penny back?' Holly wanted to believe it, but suspected Maggie was lying.

'I thought he would keep her. Force me to make another attempt. But she was waiting for me in a carrycot on the doorstep when I got home.'

Holly leaned her left arm heavily on the banister but kept the Browning on the door. 'Have you heard from him since?'

'No more messages. But why d'you think I keep this gun in the drawer?'

'What were his last words to you?'

'What I said. He told me to get out of the house. I tried to message him when I got back to my car, but he'd immediately disconnected the number.'

'This is the truth?'

'Yes,' Maggie answered without hesitation.

'Was Penny harmed in any way?'

'No. I checked her all over. She needed changing, was still wearing the same diaper I put on her the day she was taken. That was a relief to me…'

Holly nodded and then shook her head. Maggie was trying to sidetrack her – and succeeding. 'This doesn't alter my situation,' she said, categorically.

'But don't you see, it does?'

'*If* that's what happened to you – and there's no reason for me to believe that it was,' she continued before Maggie could object. 'What does that have to do with tonight?'

'It's your way out of this,' Maggie replied, her voice level.

'So I use the same story?'

'A similar one. Say I wasn't alone. Whatever.'

'No.' It felt all wrong to Holly. 'It doesn't make sense that he let Penny go.'

'He knew I'd never go to the police.'

'Why not?'

'Would you? Now you've seen how effortlessly he took Abigail.'

Maggie was right. The police seemed like an irrelevant concept now. Holly's thoughts weren't of justice. She just wanted her daughter back in her arms. 'He could be watching the house.' Her eyes slid to the black landing window again.

'If he'd been watching, do you think he would have allowed me to go into the house?'

'But perhaps the reason he released Penny was because he knew for sure you were telling the truth.' Holly chided herself. She was beginning to be sucked into Maggie's story.

'I hadn't considered that.'

Holly was dubious. Maggie had had time to consider everything. 'And you never saw this man?'

'Not then'

'When?'

'Maybe in a parking lot. The day Penny was taken.'

Holly's hands felt hot in the gloves. 'What did he look like?'

'I can't be sure it was him but there was a guy who took off in an orange Subaru. Twenties, medium build, had a weird slit in his nose.'

'You're making this up.' Holly straightened.

'Why would I? Anyway, I told you it might not have been him. He only communicated with me through the phone.'

Holly needed to lower her arm. It was getting tired.

'But I'm thinking maybe this is connected to what's been happening in Rockport,' Maggie continued.

Holly's mind tumbled the name a few times before she realised what Maggie was talking about. 'The East County Slayer? Those murders on the news?'

'They still haven't caught anyone.'

'But no children have been kidnapped… or harmed.'

'No, but all the victims were single mothers.'

Holly tried to recall the details. All she knew was that two women had been fatally stabbed.

Penny started to cry again.

CHAPTER ELEVEN

Holly focussed on the split wood of the door. Penny sounded like she was struggling for breath. 'She OK in there?'

'Doctor says it's an allergy. I worry it might be asthma.'

'I thought Abigail had a bad reaction to dust mites, but it turned out to be the paint I'd used in the nursery. She on any medication for it?' Holly asked.

'There's Zyrtec in the nursery.'

Holly glanced back at the room. 'You want me to go fetch it?'

Penny kept snuffling but Maggie said nothing.

'Did you hear me?'

'Yes. She's fine,' Maggie replied, brusquely.

Holly felt anger balloon. 'Jesus, I'm trying to help her.'

Maggie didn't respond.

'Sounds like she needs it. Look, I won't try anything.'

'She'll be OK.'

'Let me go get it. I'll pass it in through the door. You'll only have to open it a crack.' Holly reversed a pace to the nursery.

'Don't waste your time. I'm not opening it.'

'But she sounds like she's having real trouble.'

'She'll be fine,' Maggie said finally.

Holly rubbed her face. To Maggie she was nothing but a threat, the enemy and a monster. 'I don't want Penny to suffer.'

'Then leave.'

'You know I can't do that.' The gun felt heavy in Holly's hand.

'*I did*. And I have my daughter back.'

Holly so wanted Maggie's story to be true. But even if Babysitter had relieved her from killing Janet Braun, Holly had still been sent to silence *her*.

'What are your alternatives? You going to sit out there until sunrise? No. And I'm not coming out until I'm a hundred per cent positive you're gone. So, at some point, you're going to try and get inside my bedroom, and I'm going to shoot you as soon as you do.'

Holly raised her arm and pointed the Browning at Maggie's voice but it was difficult to calculate if she was directly in front of the door. *If she tried to shoot her through it, would she also maim or even kill Penny?* She couldn't live with herself if she harmed an innocent child. And if she fired and missed, Maggie would know she had a gun and be ready for her when she entered. She would have the cover of the bed and have her barrel trained on Holly as soon as she did.

'Or you can message him right now. Tell him… tell him I called the cops. Tell him I'm locked up here and they're on their way. Ask *him* what to do. He's the one who sent you here.'

Maggie was going to do anything to avoid the confrontation neither of them wanted. But Holly had to concede that maybe it was a legitimate way of playing for time. 'OK.' She imagined Maggie's weapon aimed at the panel and turned her back against the banister to take out her phone.

'Are you going back out of the nursery window?'

Holly frowned. 'Why?'

'Because your phone's in the car.' But Maggie's sceptical tone said she knew it wasn't.

Holly didn't react but tapped a message to Babysitter.

Maggie Walsh has locked herself in her bedroom and called the police.

'So what's your next move?' Maggie demanded.

Holly continued to ignore her while she waited. The phone buzzed in her hand.

Where's the child?

In the room with her.

Maggie had gone quiet. Holly assumed she knew what she was doing.

You've still got plenty of time, Holly. Figure something out.

Cold, heavy dread clambered over her. Her fingers rippled over the keys.

The police will arrive very soon.

Surely he wouldn't want her captured if she hadn't disposed of Maggie?

She won't call the police.

Holly knew he was right but she had to play ignorant.

Am panicking. Need to leave.

Holly counted the seconds while she anticipated his decision.

Maggie shifted around the bedroom; board creaking and soft thumps as she patted Penny's back.

Holly's phone vibrated.

You don't look very panicked…

CHAPTER TWELVE

Holly swivelled to the long landing window behind her and the blackness beyond. 'He's watching us.'

Maggie's motion briefly halted. 'How d'you know?'

Holly turned her back to the pane again, and then heard Maggie jerking the curtains closed. The phone buzzed twice in her hand.

Cops not coming.

Sunrise.

'We can forget all about lying to him. He knows exactly what's going on.'

'How do you know?' Sounded like Maggie and Penny were the far side of the room.

'Says he can see me.' It could have been a bluff. But if he'd allowed Maggie to have her child back after her breaking and entering at Janet Braun's place, maybe he'd seen exactly what had happened there.

Maggie said nothing. But Holly knew she had to be thinking exactly the same as her. They were in the same position as they'd been when Maggie had first locked herself behind the bedroom door. Maggie had to die to allow Abigail to live or the older mother would kill Holly to save Penny and her own life.

Holly pocketed her cell and aimed the Browning at the panel, her left hand clasping and steadying her wrist. Maggie was walking with Penny again. The board under the door groaned. *Was she now in front of it?* Holly waited for the noise to come again.

She'd be holding Penny at the same height as the gun though. *Should she aim low for her legs?* With her disabled it would make getting into the room less risky. She might drop Penny though.

Holly's finger was clammy against the trigger. All she had to do was squeeze gently like her father taught her. Just wait for the board…

Holly held the moment inside her, clenched herself around it and thought about Abigail, lying in a strange, cold place with her diaper full and Babysitter's hands gripping her tight.

The board squeaked again.

Holly closed her eyes and willed herself to release everything she was holding inside. Tears welled up, and their warmth blinded her. She only had to move one tiny muscle in her finger. She lowered the barrel an inch and waited for the board again.

It creaked.

Holly gasped, and the weapon was at her side again. She couldn't do it. Had known she'd never be able to. The tears darted down her cheeks. They were for Abigail.

'What's happening?' There was suspicion in Maggie's question.

Everything tumbled silently out of Holly.

'Speak to me.'

Holly shook her head, her mouth open and soundless. *Was he watching her now?*

'You know this is hopeless.' Maggie was still trying to break Holly down.

Penny bawled , but Holly only heard Abigail. She raised the gun from her side again.

'Talk to Babysitter. Tell him I'm not coming out.'

The board squealed.

Two shots were discharged, one swiftly after the other.

Holly felt one of the bullets strike her and was instantly looking at the landing ceiling.

CHAPTER THIRTEEN

It sounded like Penny was crying in a different room. Her sobbing was drowned by hissing and Maggie could only imagine how the gunshots had affected her baby's tiny eardrums. She lifted her off the bed and hugged her soft, cool cheek against her face. 'I'm so sorry, sweetheart,' she whispered. Maggie examined the two holes in the split door and tried to pick up any sounds of pain from the other side. But Penny's wailing and her deadened hearing made it impossible to work out if any of the bullets had struck the woman.

'Ssshhh.' Maggie rocked Penny and covered her little ears, but she was inconsolable.

A short dragging noise from the landing.

Maggie stroked Penny's head. 'Ssshhh.' She couldn't discern anything else, so bent her knees and looked through one of the holes. Only the half-open nursery door was visible.

A grunt.

Maggie squinted but then suddenly stood. If she hadn't injured her then it was likely she'd provoked an assault in return. Maggie carried Penny to the other side of the room so she had the bed between them and the door. She crouched down at the end of the mattress so only her head would be visible if the intruder looked through the same holes. There were five bullets in the gun so only three left. 'Ssshhh.' She kept caressing Penny's ears. 'If you can… leave now!' she yelled at the panel. But she needed an answer. Had to know if she was lying out there or had darted to one of the other rooms. 'Come near this door and I'll do the same again!'

No response.

Maggie swallowed a few times but a high-pitched whine trickled into her ears. 'Speak to me!' Maggie frowned as she struggled to make out a reply.

She turned quickly to the window behind her. She'd drawn the curtains over it. Babysitter couldn't see into the room, and her head was lower than the ledge.

Maggie had to stay where she was, not be tempted to return to the door until she knew what had happened. 'I can't call you an ambulance. There'd be too many questions. I can tell you where my first aid kit is though.!'

Penny's chest heaved against Maggie. *Had she done permanent damage to her daughter's hearing? But that was something she'd worry about when she'd removed her from the danger outside. What if the woman died? Had Mrs Serafina heard the shots? She was deaf but perhaps one of the other neighbours was calling the cops. If they arrived, she'd just have to convince them it was a random burglary.*

If a patrol car didn't turn up, what would she do? Get rid of the body herself? The prospect made her shudder. She couldn't even begin to imagine how she'd accomplish that. But the last week had taught her exactly what she was capable of when Penny's life was at stake.

Her daughter's eyes were still screwed tight. Tears glistened on her red cheeks, and the distress distorting her face seemed more intense than when she'd first pulled the trigger. Penny's pain was Maggie's, and she'd been responsible. 'Soon it won't hurt any more. I promise. It'll go away.'

But would her attacker? Surely Penny's bawling would act as a reminder of the woman's child and what Babysitter had threatened if she didn't kill Maggie.

A low thud. Like somebody butting a wall.

'Are you hurt?' It seemed a ludicrous question to ask the person she might have just shot. Maggie cocked her head away from Penny. The woman could be bleeding out on the landing. *Could Maggie let her die there? But if she refused to communicate how could she help her?*

And if she hadn't been shot and was still mobile Maggie had given her a good reason to carry out what she'd come to do. This could all be a bluff. She could just be waiting for Maggie to unlock the door.

Another, softer, impact.

'Just let me know! I'm not coming out until you have!'

Penny struggled against her shouting. Maybe any sound would hurt her now.

The woman was obviously still alive. *But how long would that be the case?* Maggie stroked Penny's fine yellow hair. 'Everything's fine.'

CHAPTER FOURTEEN

Holly used her heels to push her spine further up the wall behind her. She was sitting on the carpet, peering down at the dark stain on the blue waterproof material of her poncho. She didn't want to lift it to look, but knew she had to. Her scalp prickled cold, and she wondered if she was going to pass out.

Penny's crying was like a tiny voice of her own distress.

She could feel warmth where the bullet had struck her but no pain. Just an odd buzzing sensation. *Was she in shock?* She could scarcely feel her buttocks on the floor. *Had the slug hit her spine?* She wiggled her toes in her boots.

'Say something!'

Holly was in no hurry to answer Maggie. She gritted her teeth and lifted the edge of her poncho and then her black pullover. She sucked in breath as she saw the large red patch above the waistband of her jeans, soaking through the olive green material of her T-shirt. She tugged it clear and exposed the skin with a black slit surrounded by shiny blood. It was just beside the top of her left hipbone. *Had it gone in and ruptured anything vital?*

'Oh, Jesus.' Holly felt nausea break over her. She tried to sit up further and, as she did, fresh blood poured out of the wound. It seemed so black. She ran her rubber-sheathed fingers across her stomach but couldn't see another one. 'Oh, Christ,' she muttered. Her fingertips smeared red over her skin.

What was she supposed to do? She knew nothing about bullet injuries. The iciness spread to her forehead, and she focussed on the bedroom door. She could see the two holes in the panel. If

Maggie wanted to take any more pot-shots at her she was still in the line of fire. Her own weapon lay only a couple of feet away from her left boot.

Beside her was the half-open door to the bathroom. Holly put her palms against the floor to shift herself sideways to it and yelped when the action pumped more blood out of her.

'I can hear you there.'

Holly figured the sooner she was off the landing the better. She turned her body so her back was to the bathroom door and reversed on her behind. She leaned over and grabbed the handgun and droplets of blood sprayed over the mushroom carpet. She buffeted the door on her way through, and it jarred her, amplifying the fizz in her hip.

She slid all the way into the room and closed the door, pointing her weapon at it immediately after. If Maggie knew she was injured she might make the most of the opportunity and come in to finish her off.

But as her breathing slowed Penny's muffled crying still hadn't ceased. As long as the sound remained the same she knew Maggie was behind the bedroom door.

She slid all the way into the corner so she was between the side of the bath and the sink, with the hand towel against the back of her head. There were droplets of her blood on the tiles in her wake. So much for not leaving any tell-tale DNA behind.

The room settled, and she tried to slow her breathing. Holly felt so hot and needed to remove her hat. But she figured she might be able to clean the blood up. She left her hair tucked away and blew some air into her face before looking at her watch.

11:05 p.m.

Less than eight hours until sunrise.

Had she briefly lost consciousness after she'd been shot? She couldn't remember falling, only sitting up and retreating towards the nursery. *Could she still leave the house a murderer?*

Maggie would do anything to protect Penny. *Shouldn't she be as ruthless and, if she wasn't, didn't that mean she was doing less to save her own daughter?* Looking at her blood smeared over the floor, however, Holly felt the beginnings of anger soaking through.

Maggie's two bullets had been aimed directly at her. Holly had hesitated and now she wouldn't. If Maggie had opened fire so readily it was less likely she could believe her story about Babysitter allowing her to have Penny back when she hadn't killed Janet Braun.

She lifted her T-shirt again. The waistband of her jeans was saturated. Was she going to bleed out? She had to get to the first aid kit Maggie had mentioned. Or would that be another trick to misdirect her? Whether it was or not, the wound needed dressing now. If the bullet had fatally injured her there was nothing she could do. If not, Holly had to attend to it. She couldn't deal with Maggie if she didn't.

Penny was still howling, and she could hear her mother trying to console her. The discharge must have been pretty loud in there. *Had Maggie really meant to kill Holly, or were the shots just a demonstration that she had the gun and was deadly serious about defending her child?* But she hadn't aimed low, like Holly had been considering. Both holes in the door had been at waist height.

If neighbours called the police, she would be taken in, sunrise would come and go, and she'd never see Abigail again. She had to use that to put herself back on her feet and to follow through with the instructions she'd been given. As far as Maggie was concerned, Holly only had a carving knife. That gave her an edge, and perhaps what she should be doing was further convincing Maggie of that until she was given the right moment to use her bullets.

CHAPTER FIFTEEN

'Tell me where the first aid kit is!' Holly had taken a look around the bathroom, but the slim mirror cabinet wasn't big enough to contain it.

Penny's bellowing didn't let up, but Holly heard the floorboard creak by the bedroom door.

'Are you badly hurt?' Maggie asked from behind it.

'First aid kit!' Despite the blood, it didn't look like a bullet had entered, just grazed her.

'Best thing you can do is get to the hospital.'

Holly wiped cold sweat from her eyebrow.

'You can say somebody mugged you in the street.'

'I'm not leaving! We can talk but I need that kit now!'

Holly could almost hear Maggie's brain churning.

'OK, downstairs in the kitchen above the stove. You'll have to unlock the door. Bolt at the top and bottom.'

But if she went down there would Maggie make an escape bid? She figured it was better to move stealthily while Penny was still yelling. Sliding herself forward she immediately flinched and looked down at her wound weeping more blood onto the tiles. The buzzing was giving way to raw pain now. The shock must rapidly be wearing off.

Holly pushed herself back to the door on her butt and pulled it open.

Penny wasn't calming down, and the bedroom door was still firmly closed. Holly looked across the landing to the top of the stairs. She could shimmy over and carefully descend, maybe without Maggie hearing her. The bolts were another matter but, hopefully, by then she would have gotten enough of a head start.

Then she saw the two bullet holes in the plaster at the far edge of the nursery door and felt a surge of relief. Neither was inside her.

She aimed her Browning at the bedroom. *Should she fire a warning shot at it?* That would probably ensure Maggie wouldn't come out. But Holly didn't want her to know she had the gun until the right moment.

She kept it directed at the door. Maggie could be watching her through the bullet holes. Holly extended her legs from the bathroom onto the landing and hastily dragged herself to the top of the stairs and dropped down so she was sitting on the second one. Even though she only landed gently the impact accentuated the pain now jaggedly palpitating against the waist of her jeans. She restrained an exclamation and wondered if she should loosen her button. It felt like her skin was caught on barbed wire.

She had to move fast before Maggie started another dialogue and realised she wasn't in the bathroom. Holly took her weight onto her wrists and delicately lifted herself down to the next step, clenching her jaw tight and hoping the old wood didn't give her away.

Holly was almost at the bottom when it creaked. She froze and looked back up to the landing. Penny was still crying herself sick but she wondered if Maggie had picked up the vibrations of Holly moving down the stairs. She waited a few seconds, seeing if the sound of Penny's sobbing would change as Maggie moved across the room to the door, but it didn't. Whether Maggie knew what she was doing or not, there was no point in hesitating.

She pocketed the Browning. *Should she remove the gloves?* One was covered in her blood. She didn't want to leave fingerprints as well, though, and decided against it. Putting the soles of her boots on the amber carpet of the dimly lit downstairs lounge Holly pushed herself off the stairs and into a standing position. She could feel the blood from the top half of her body heavy on the wound and felt suddenly woozy. Then she clocked her carving knife lying a few feet in front of her. Sorely snatching it up Holly staggered, wiped her tacky glove on her poncho and rested her shoulder on the doorframe, steadying herself and letting the dizziness subside. She hoped there were plenty of super strength painkillers in Maggie's first aid kit.

Stretching her arm to the little brass bolt at the top of the door Holly felt the action tug at the wound. She barely gulped back a groan and quickly fumbled for the metal. It was lodged firmly in the frame. She waited, muscle trembling under her armpit, and attempted to cover the action of snapping it back by timing it with Penny's wails.

Holly tried to ease the bolt, but it shot out hard. There was no way Maggie wouldn't have heard.

Holly crouched and quickly freed the bottom bolt. That one wasn't as loud but now it didn't matter. She turned the handle, stepped into the generous kitchen and switched on the light. She limped over to the stove, dumping the knife on the flattop as she reached up to open the narrow door over the range hood.

Maggie hadn't been lying. There was a white zip-up first aid bag inside. She tugged it out and hobbled back to the door, taking out her gun and pointing it up the stairs. She hadn't heard the bedroom door open, and there was no sign of movement on the landing.

Penny's blubbing was slowing now.

Holly set the bag on the breakfast bar and frantically unzipped it to examine the contents. She confirmed there were dressings and Band-Aids and found some painkillers at the bottom. She walked back into the lounge to check on the stairs again.

She halted as she noticed, in the light from the kitchen, the cluster of framed photographs on the dresser in front of her – images of Penny as a baby, some taken of her in a professional studio and others with Maggie in shot. There were also pictures of Maggie with a man.

Holly registered he didn't appear in any of the photos of Penny. *Was he the father or had the relationship ended before Maggie was pregnant?* She quickly scanned the rest of the room. The decor was very feminine. No masculine clothing hanging from the hooks inside the front door. Zero signs of male habitation.

She'd assumed Maggie lived alone when she'd watched the place. *And would Babysitter really have sent Holly to kill her if there was a man in the house?* Maggie had walked in on Janet Braun with someone else there though. But it sounded like that had been bad timing. If she was to believe her story at all.

A click and the door shuddering from overhead. Penny had fallen silent.

Holly turned to the stairs and saw Maggie's bare feet appear at the top. She darted back into the kitchen, partially closed the door behind her and aimed her handgun out through the gap. Maggie hadn't been able to see her from that angle. Wouldn't know she had the Browning.

'You should leave now,' Maggie said firmly. 'Take the things you need and go. The key to the back door is in the dish by the microwave.'

Holly's eyes shifted to it and back to the stairs. 'How do I know you won't shoot me from the window when I'm walking up the alley?' She had to give Maggie the impression she was going to flee.

'You have my word,' Maggie reassured her.

Was she still holding Penny? The baby was quiet so it was impossible to tell. Again, if she stood at the bottom of the stairs and fired up at her would she hit the child? Or might Maggie drop her down the stairs? But surely she wouldn't have brought Penny into their confrontation. She had to have left her in the bedroom.

But Holly reminded herself that Maggie believed she only had a knife. It was what Babysitter had told Maggie to use on Janet Braun.

'Tell Babysitter what we discussed. That you can't get to me,' Maggie's voice quavered. 'I'm not letting you back up here now. I'll shoot you if you come near these stairs. You know I will.'

Holly didn't doubt it. 'You really think he'll let Abigail go free if I let you live?'

'You don't have the power to let me live. I'm just telling you what you have to do if *you* want to.'

Momentarily, Holly felt nothing but admiration for Maggie. She had to be as terrified as she was but was unwavering in shielding Penny from harm. Holly wished she were as resolute. And in that moment she took strength from it, flicked the safety off and stepped from the cover of the kitchen door.

She raised the Browning and took two paces to the foot of the stairs. The bottom half of Maggie's body came into view.

Holly pointed the barrel squarely at her. And Penny.

CHAPTER SIXTEEN

Maggie got her first proper look at the woman's face as it appeared at the bottom of the stairs, outlined by a dark woollen hat. Then she realised it was behind the barrel of a gun that was pointing directly at her and Penny.

There was no time to fire her own; only protect her daughter. She spun away from the top, twisting her body as she anticipated the sound of the shot and the bullet slamming into her.

But the woman hesitated, and Maggie was able to get Penny out of the line of fire and rush back to the bedroom. She slammed the swollen door after two attempts and swiftly locked it, reversing quickly to her position behind the bed again. She lay Penny down on the carpet behind it. 'Just rest there a minute, sweetheart.'

She gripped Jeff's snubbie revolver with both shaking hands and held it on the door, her elbows on the mattress. Maggie waited for the thumps on the stairs as the woman followed, but couldn't hear anything.

Penny spluttered beside her.

'Ssshhh, everything's all right.' But it wasn't. If the woman had a firearm then Maggie didn't have the upper hand. She could just as easily shoot Maggie through the door. 'It's OK, honey.' At least now she had the measure of the other mother. She appeared to be in her early twenties and it didn't look as if the injury Maggie had inflicted was serious enough to make her leave. She was as determined as Maggie. *How badly was she wounded? Or had that been a ploy to lure Maggie out of the bedroom?* She'd seen spots of blood on the landing carpet though. 'Don't come up here!' she shouted and strained for a response. She had to find out exactly where the woman was.

No reply. The whining in her ear had begun to fade, and she tried to pick up signs of her moving about, but the house was silent except for Penny's laboured breathing. Then another noise drew her attention to the window behind her.

The swish of tyres on snow. They halted outside the house and car doors opened and shut. *Was it safe to peer out of the window?* Maggie went to the right side of the frame and craned around the curtain without disturbing it.

It was a patrol car. *Shit. Who had called them?* Maggie watched two officers surveying the street. She couldn't see their faces because the peaks of their dark caps concealed them.

One of them glanced up at the window, and she leaned back quickly, even though she wasn't visible. Looked like they were definitely calling on her.

She waited, hoping the melody she was dreading wouldn't come.

But it did.

The woman was the first to react to the doorbell. 'It's the police,' she hissed up the stairs.

Maggie circled back around the bed but hesitated at the right-hand side of the door. 'I have to answer it, or they might come round back.'

'Is it locked?'

'Yes.'

'Then let's wait for them to leave.'

'Somebody must have reported the gunshots.'

'You?'

'I think we've already established it wasn't.'

The bell rang again.

Maggie chewed her lip. 'I can send them away.'

There was a brief silence. 'If you alert them to what's going on—'

'If I wanted to, I would have called them. Go into the kitchen and close the door behind you. I'm bringing Penny down. If you try anything, they're going to hear your gunshot. So even if you do get Abigail back you'll be spending her life in prison.'

A fist thumped the front door.

'OK, I'm going but I'll be listening to every word from there. Give me away and you won't make it out of the house.'

Maggie swallowed. There was no other choice. 'Hide yourself. We're coming down.'

CHAPTER SEVENTEEN

Holly retreated to the kitchen, pushed the door closed but left it cracked. 'OK, you'd better hurry.' She heard Maggie open the bedroom door then come down the stairs and aimed her Browning through the gap. But she knew Maggie wouldn't surprise her, not with Penny in her arms and the police standing outside.

Maggie reached the bottom of the stairs, and the door was suddenly pulled shut.

Holly lunged for the handle, but it was too late. The top bolt slid quickly into place. 'Open this!'

'Just a precaution. I'll unlock it when they're gone.'

Holly bit down on her anger. She doubted that but couldn't yell at her now.

'Stay quiet.'

Knuckles rapped on the door.

'Just answer it,' Holly snarled. She kept her weapon on the panel but backed away a few paces. Then she could make out Maggie crossing the lounge and unlocking the front door.

'Officers?' Maggie faked grogginess.

'Sorry, ma'am,' apologised one of them. 'Did we wake you?'

'I was up with my daughter, and we were just getting back to sleep.'

'We've had a report that a shot was heard from this address,' said the other, whose voice was younger and a little more businesslike.

'A shot?'

'Yes. Did you hear anything?'

'No. Are we talking about a gun?' There was believable alarm in Maggie's reaction.

Holly guessed she had her gun in the pocket of her robe.

'Don't be alarmed,' reassured the first voice. 'We just have to check these things out. It could have been a car backfiring.'

'Are you alone here, ma'am?' enquired the other.

'Yes. Except for this one.'

'Hello, sweetie,' the first babytalked to Penny. 'You're looking a bit dazed. Don't be scared, honey.'

'Say hi to the officers,' Maggie whispered.

Holly put her ear closer to the door.

'How old is she?' the first asked.

'Eighteen months.'

'Got two myself. Given up on sleep. Second has picked up the baton from the first.'

'I think she needs to be fed,' Maggie explained. 'Don't you, Penny? Gonna make Mommy sore again?'

Nice touch, Holly thought. She looked down at her boot and saw the spots of blood on the toe. Momentarily, she'd forgotten her injury.

Neither of the officers responded.

'Do you want to come in?'

'No, that's fine. I think your neighbour was more eager to know you're OK.' The first seemed happy with the situation.

'If it was Mrs Serafina then I know she can be a little jumpy. She's eighty-four, and her husband died last year.'

'Maybe we'll just take a quick look around.' The second wasn't ready to leave. 'Just as a precaution.'

'Sure.'

'Can we access the yard down the side?' His boots crunched on snow as he took a few steps back.

Holly turned to the window behind her and the darkened yard beyond. The falling flakes were vaguely lit by the glow of a string of solar-powered fairy lights in a tree.

'Yeah. Just open the gate. Are you actually looking for somebody then?' The trepidation was back in Maggie's delivery.

Holly considered what a good actor she was. *How much of what she'd told her about Janet Braun had been a performance?*

'No, no. As we're here… My fellow officer likes to be thorough, ma'am.' The first sounded irked. 'Nothing to be alarmed about.'

'OK. Can I get you both some coffee?'

Don't push it, Holly thought.

'No, we're good, thanks, ma'am,' the second answered.

'Apparently so.' The irritation hadn't left the first's voice.

'OK. I'll leave you to it. You might want to look in on Mrs Serafina next door. I'm sure she'll want to know what's going on.'

'We will do. And we should be out of here soon,' the first promised.

'OK if I close this?'

'Sure, and sorry for disturbing you.'

'No problem. Just doing your job.'

'Bye bye, sweetie. Take care of your mom.'

'Say goodbye…' Maggie kept her voice steady.

The front door closed and was locked before Maggie padded back to the kitchen.

'Open this now.' Holly booted the door.

'You'll have to hide first. They're coming around back.'

The officers' boots clumped past the alley wall to her left, and then a flashlight flitted across the white lawn. She left the light on but crouched behind the breakfast bar.

'Are you out of sight?' Maggie was right by the door now.

'Yes.' Holly's grip tightened on the handle of her Browning. She could shoot Maggie through the panel, as she'd done to her. But the officers would definitely know about it. She had to wait until they left.

'Come on, Reynolds.' The first officer was still peeved.

The second officer didn't answer him.

Holly peered over the counter and beyond the dried flower arrangement on the windowsill and saw the yard illuminated. The beam arced around the snowflakes, and the first officer appeared and stood with his back to the kitchen window.

He sighed. 'Let's go next door and see if this old girl's all right.'

Holly looked at her watch but didn't register the time. How long were they going to be around? She darted her head back to the door expecting Maggie to be standing there. But the bolt was in place. It would crack if she tried to come in.

'Can't see anything.' The second officer joined the first.

'Really?' the first said sardonically. 'Come on. You get on the radio, and I'll go speak to the old lady.'

They traipsed back along the alley to the front of the house. Holly immediately relocated to the other side of the breakfast bar and pointed her gun at the door with both hands. She could still pick up their voices at the front of the house, then low thumps as they knocked the neighbour's door.

'Wait.' Maggie's voice was right by the panel.

She still had Penny in her arms. But this might be the only chance Holly had of a shot. The first officer greeted Maggie's neighbour. *How long would they take to leave?*

Holly's finger rested gently on the trigger.

CHAPTER EIGHTEEN

As it rolled back out of Bozeman Street Holly didn't wait for the patrol car's engine to fade. 'Unbolt this door.' Now they'd left, the pain at her hip recommenced with a new intensity.

There was no movement from the lounge. *Had Maggie retreated upstairs with Penny?*

'The door to the yard's right there; you can leave now.' Maggie's voice didn't sound as close as it had.

Holly steadied her Browning at the door. 'Open it.'

'No. I'm sitting at the bottom of the stairs. Fire away. We're shielded by the wall.'

'Then I'll just have to take my chances. If I boot it down are you really willing to risk Penny's life?'

'I open it, you try to kill me. I leave it locked, you try to kill me. We have to figure this out.'

Holly hooked the strap of the first aid bag with the barrel of her gun and slid it towards her.

'We've both had our children threatened, and the only solution we can see is doing what's been demanded of us.'

Holly burst a few painkillers out of their blister pack and swallowed them dry. 'So what's the other?' She wondered how hard she'd have to kick the door to break the little brass bolt.

'Do we really know that Babysitter is watching the house?'

Holly recalled her exchange with him. He hadn't said anything that convinced her a hundred per cent. 'What difference does it make?'

'If he is, he has to have seen the police arrive. Wouldn't that be a perfect excuse for you to abort this? And you can tell him you're injured.'

She was right. Babysitter hadn't believed the cops would show up. It had to be worth trying. Holly pulled her iPhone out of her back pocket.

'If he's the East County Slayer he won't want the police knowing the truth. What d'you think?'

'Just wait.' Holly quickly tapped a message. She got sticky blood from her rubber-sheathed fingers on the screen.

Have been shot. Police arrived at house. Neighbour called them. Sent them away but they seemed suspicious. Maggie still locked behind door.

Holly sent it. 'You think he could really be the Slayer?'

'Maybe he didn't attack any of them. Perhaps it's all down to people like us.'

Holly hadn't had any time to consider the connection that Maggie had hinted at earlier. 'So you kill Janet, I kill you... somebody kills me.'

'Means Babysitter never gets his hands dirty. But everyone thinks it's one killer. Each murderer only conceals their part for a couple of days before the next silences them. And they spend that brief time just grateful to have their child back.'

'But why?' Holly kept her eyes on her phone screen.

'I don't know. But when Penny was abducted, I might have almost stopped him in the parking lot.'

CHAPTER NINETEEN

Maggie had been in Hatchet Park Shopping Mall the day Babysitter kidnapped Penny. He hadn't grabbed her from the pram. He'd taken the whole thing. In broad daylight. One moment it had been outside the stall as she'd used the public bathroom, the front wheels visible under the door as she quickly peed. Then she'd heard somebody come in. She only became suspicious when nobody entered one of the other stalls. 'Hello?' Maggie had waited for a reply or further footsteps.

That's when the wheels of Penny's pram sped from sight. Maggie still had her panties around her ankles but sprang up as her exclamation echoed around the stall.

She unlocked the door and found the bathroom empty. Hitching up her skirt she crossed the tiles to the exit and looked into the outside lot beyond. No sign of anyone pushing the pram.

As she contemplated the rows of cars in the large mall parking zone Maggie felt as if she'd just hit the ground floor in a falling elevator. 'Penny!' There wasn't a soul in evidence, and her eyes darted between the vehicle spaces for signs of movement. 'Penny!' Her insides churned.

An engine started up, and she tried to pinpoint which area of the lot it was. Advancing on the lines of cars she cut through the first, trying to see through the windshields before heading for the next.

It sounded like it was some way in front of her, and Maggie crossed three more rows before she saw a dark blue Audi pulling out. She shot to the left end and tried to block its departure, and the car screeched to a standstill a foot away from her. There was a child in the back seat but Maggie could immediately tell it wasn't Penny strapped into the chair.

The mother in the front berated her, but Maggie was already scouring the other bays. Then she spotted another vehicle crawling along the right edge of the parking zone. She could just see its silver roof as it glided by the other cars.

The exit was just behind Maggie. She turned her back on the Audi and raced to the ramp to block its path. The mother behind her honked but Maggie kept her gaze fixed on the silver Toyota as it reached the end of the row and turned to face her.

As it approached, Maggie couldn't see through the tinted windshield but planted herself in the middle of the road so it had to drive right through her to escape.

The car braked about thirty feet away from her. *Was Penny in there?* Her attention shifted to the other cars but she couldn't see any more vehicles leaving.

The mother blasted her horn to the left of Maggie several times. She wanted to make a right for the exit, but Maggie stood her ground and waited for the silver Toyota to move.

It backed up, and Maggie strode towards it. *Was it the person who had taken Penny or was the driver simply reacting to her erratic behaviour?* Maggie kept covering the distance between them as the car halted at the perimeter hedge.

It waited for her, and Maggie's pace speeded up. *Would they drive straight at her?* She didn't care. Even if she sustained injury, she wouldn't allow them to leave.

Another engine gunned, and her head shot briefly to where a car was pulling out of its spot four rows away from her. It was orange and seemed in a hurry. Maggie heard the mother's Audi exit behind her but now the Toyota blared its horn.

The orange car stopped a few feet behind it, almost pranging it, and joined in the cacophony.

Maggie was only ten feet from the silver Toyota and was straining to see through the windshield.

But the orange car suddenly reversed the way it had come. It was going to circle around, and she no longer had the exit covered. She watched it turn and accelerate along the rear row. *Could Penny be inside that one?*

The silver Toyota blew its horn at her again, and she walked swiftly backwards towards the exit to block both cars.

The orange car shot down the rows towards the exit. Maggie turned away from the Toyota. She was still obstructing its escape so she dashed back to the ramp.

The orange car skidded and froze as she ran into its path. It was a Subaru, and its male owner dropped his window.

'What d'you think you're doing? I could have killed you.' He looked to be in his mid-twenties.

Maggie craned to see his face as he half leaned out of the window then looked over her shoulder at the Toyota. It hadn't budged.

'Get out the way.'

Maggie took in his shaved head and stubble but it was his nose that was his most conspicuous feature. It looked like a blade had split one of his nostrils. 'Who's with you in the car?'

'What the hell are you talking about?'

Maggie took two steps nearer but couldn't see anyone else inside. *Could Penny be in the trunk?* 'My baby has been taken. Please turn your engine off, just for a moment.' She checked the silver Toyota but it was still motionless.

The driver's face softened. 'What? Wait.' He killed the engine.

'I can't allow anyone to leave.'

'Your baby?' The driver took out his phone. 'You want me to call the cops?'

Maggie nodded and backed away towards the exit again so neither car could get by.

The silver Toyota's engine was switched off, its door opened, and a balding man in a tan suit got out. He was squat and didn't have a neck. 'What the fuck is your problem?' He shouted over and raised his short arms in exasperation.

Maggie held up her hands. 'Please.' But she was surveying the other cars in the lot. Maybe neither of these guys had Penny.

The squat guy stalked towards her. 'If you don't get out of the way, I'll call the cops.'

'I'm already calling them.' The orange Subaru driver had a phone to his ear. 'Her baby's been snatched.'

The Toyota owner deflated. 'Snatched?'

Maggie was still inspecting the other cars. No others were moving, but it didn't mean someone wasn't sitting inside one biding their time.

'They're on their way.' The driver of the orange Subaru hadn't got out.

The silver Toyota owner attempted to mould his face into concern. 'Look, I appreciate you've got a situation here but I've got clients waiting.'

Maggie examined the tall hedges that demarcated the lot. The only way out for cars was the entry and exit ramps. *But could there be openings that would allow someone to escape on foot with the pram?*

'Sir, didn't you hear me?' The orange Subaru driver opened his door. 'We're talking about a baby here.'

Their arguing was drowned by the sound of her accelerated circulation. 'She was in a pram. Somebody just took it while I was in the bathroom.' She glimpsed a head moving at the back of the parking zone. It was a woman pushing something. But when she stood on tiptoes she could see it was a shopping cart.

'All right, all right.' The silver Toyota owner had his hands on his hips, and craned around. He was shorter than she was.

'Penny!' She screamed it now and waited, but there was no response, no crying. She could feel the weight of her alarm like a rock in her stomach.

'I'll take this side,' the orange Subaru driver said to the Toyota driver. 'You check that way.'

'I really gotta be somewhere.'

'Jesus, is it really *that* important?'

Maggie felt queasy. A voice told her that Penny was long gone. That whatever anybody did now was too late. But they couldn't have got far. Maggie left the two arguing drivers at the exit and ran. She pumped her arms and followed the hedge around, looking for an escape route while simultaneously scrutinising each row of cars.

She came to the mother loading up her shopping and turned along the rear hedge. No way out there. Behind it was a brick wall.

Maggie turned the corner and ran down the side of the lot to the exit. Then she saw Penny's pram. It was up against a barrier in an empty bay. She heard wheels screech and pelted back to find the Toyota driver alone.

'Where did he go?'

'Took off.'

Maggie heard blood rushing through her ears. 'Why did you let him go?'

The thickset Toyota owner recoiled from Maggie's expression.

'We've got to drive after him!'

'But he called the cops.'

Perhaps he'd pretended to. 'Which way did he go?'

'Didn't see after he dropped down the ramp.'

'We have to follow him!' Maggie was already making for his car.

'OK. Get in,' he offered, even though he had no choice.

Maggie opened the door and dropped into the passenger seat. 'Come on, he's getting away!'

The Toyota driver swung into the vehicle. 'You're sure you're not both scamming me?'

'Drive!'

Her exclamation removed all doubt from his face. He started the Toyota again, and they lurched towards the exit. Dropping down the ramp they had to decelerate at the barrier, and he fumbled in his pocket for his ticket. 'Shit. It was here.'

Maggie scraped it up off the dash and thrust it at him. But as he inserted it into the slot, the arm raised and they pulled out into the street outside, there was no sign of the orange Subaru in either direction.

CHAPTER TWENTY

You two must be getting along just fine. I saw Maggie send the cops away. Kill her, Holly, or Abigail pays.

Holly felt the room tilt and leaned her body against the breakfast bar. Whether he was the man Maggie had seen in the parking lot or not there was no doubt Babysitter was watching. Her bloodied fingers shook as she typed her reply.

Maggie locked me in kitchen while she dealt with them. Cannot escape.

Am losing blood. she added. Even though it seemed the flow had actually stopped.

'What's going on?' Maggie sounded like she was still at the bottom of the stairs.

'Quiet!' Holly's hip radiated agony as she hoisted herself onto one of the tall stools at the bar. Grabbing some dressings from the first aid kit, she was just about to one-handedly tear a pack open using her teeth when her phone vibrated again.

You're a resourceful girl, Holly. If you leave the house by the back door there are plenty of windows to choose from to get back in. Go.

Holly's energy drained out of her boots. Now he'd seen Maggie send the officer away he probably thought they were in cahoots. The kitchen swung, and she breathed in through her nose and out through her mouth.

'Are you OK in there?'

She tried to straighten. What was she going to do now? Her forehead bristled. If she lost consciousness, Maggie could just undo the bolt and that would be the end of Abigail.

'Maybe you need a doctor.'

She flitted her gaze around the kitchen. It settled on the dried flower arrangement on the sill. Keeping the gun on the door, she pushed herself off the stool and over to the window. Holly examined the spiky egg-shaped heads among them before breaking one off the stem. She gripped it firmly in her free palm and felt the prickles dig painfully into it. *That might work.*

'Answer me.'

Holly clasped it tighter and felt the points pierce her skin. If she began to black out she could bring herself round. 'I still haven't had a reply.' She grabbed the knife off the flat-top, hobbled back to the stool and lifted herself back onto the seat.

'Listen, I know you're telling yourself you can't leave—'

Holly slid the knife into her left pocket. 'Wait.' She paused, as if absorbing something. 'He's told me to get out of here.'

Silence from the lounge.

'Police, question mark, leave now,' Holly said, as if reading from her phone.

'What are you waiting for then?' Maggie said eventually. She sounded suspicious.

'But how do I know he'll return Abigail?' Now she had to sell the lie.

'I got Penny back, didn't I?' But Maggie's voice was flat. 'Ssshhh.'

Holly realised Maggie still had Penny with her. She fought another wave of nausea and aimed her Browning at the doorway. *Was Maggie really holding her child or was she at the panel slowly shooting the bolt?* 'OK, I'm going through the back door. Stay away from the windows and don't come out front. I'll shoot if you do. Don't open the bolt until I'm gone either.'

'Deal.' Maggie said nothing else.

Slipping some dressings and the flower head in her pocket, Holly slid down from the stool again. *Now where did Maggie say she'd put the key?* She limped to the microwave and found a bunch in the bowl there. She clutched them so they wouldn't jingle and reversed to the back door, keeping her eyes and gun on the locked panel. *Why had she gone so quiet?* 'Say something!'

'What more is there for me to say?'

'Just answer me and let me know you're still where you say you are.'

'OK.' But Maggie's reply sounded muted.

Was she on her way upstairs to fire at her out of the window? Holly slid the key into the lock as quietly as she could. 'You going to try anything?'

'Just leave.'

'That's not an answer.' Holly used her retort to cover the sound of turning the key.

'Do you think I'd endanger Penny any more than I have to?'

'Still not an answer.' She pushed down on the handle.

'I promise, I'll stay right here.'

'OK – where did you say those back door keys were?' Holly pushed open the door and felt the night air cool her face. Swollen white flakes settled on her arm. It was snowing heavier than when she'd entered the house.

'By the microwave.'

'OK.' She stepped out into the yard and looked up at the pane immediately above her. No light on in the room, and the window was sealed. She put her wet face back through the doorway. 'They're not there.' But she didn't wait for Maggie's response. Holly quietly closed the door behind her, locked it, pocketed the keys then rapidly crept across the front of the kitchen window and through the open wooden gate into the alley at the side of the house.

She could hear Maggie replying from inside, but it was incoherent. Ahead of her was the side of the kitchen and two lounge windows. They both cast a weak glow against the wall the other side of the alley. From her angle she couldn't tell if the curtains were drawn in them. She tried to recall if they had been when she'd been there earlier.

Holly looked upwards to the single window of the nursery. It was still open. *Could she climb back up the drainpipe with her injury or would Maggie lean out with her gun at any moment?* She listened for sounds of activity inside. Nothing.

Maggie would know she'd left when she didn't reply, so there was no time to deliberate. She sidled along the wall until she came to the first lower window. Looked like the shutter had been closed in that one but she crouched beneath the ledge. She held in a grunt as her wound complained but shuffled across and straightened again as soon as she'd cleared it.

The alley swayed, and Holly gripped the prickles in her pocket hard. But it did nothing to dispel her light-headedness, and she leaned her back against the wall for support. She kept her gaze fixed on the end of the alley. *Maybe Maggie would come out the front door and try to intercept her there.*

She hadn't heard any sound from that direction yet but strained to listen. She had to go. Holly ducked low again and scuttled under the second shuttered window. Now she was below the nursery. She kept her eyes on its pane as she passed under the ledge. Maybe Maggie wouldn't try anything at all. All she wanted was for Holly to leave. *But wouldn't she expect her to try to kill her another time?*

She stood again and pointed the gun barrel to the blackness at the end of the alley and then back the way she'd just come. She had to get clear of the house. Stay hidden for a while until Maggie believed she'd really gone. But there was always a chance she could be ambushed on the way out.

She took a pace towards the end of the alley, but stopped in her tracks. *What the hell was that noise?*

It sounded like an insect. If it was, though, it had to have big wings. It reminded Holly of a hummingbird. She looked up and then swiftly back towards the yard again. No sight or sound of Maggie. She returned her attention to the way out of the alley and something caught her eye.

What was floating ten feet away? She blinked against the snowflakes and tried to focus. There was definitely something suspended there. *Was this a trick?* Holly could see a tiny green light bobbing steadily. Then it shot up into the air.

She looked skywards, but the green light had vanished into the blackness, and the snow was falling in her eyes again. Holly knew what it was though. A drone. That's how Babysitter was monitoring them. He'd probably been hovering it outside the windows and observing everything that had been going on between them.

And now he knew she'd left. *Would he assume she'd given up? And what did that mean for Abigail?*

CHAPTER TWENTY-ONE

It looked like the woman had left soon after she'd asked Maggie where the keys to the back door were. There had been silence since.

Settling Penny carefully on the couch and keeping her snubbie in one hand, Maggie knelt beside the kitchen door to listen. Nothing. It could have been a trap to get her to unbolt it, but she wasn't about to do that. She doubted Babysitter had let the woman leave before the job was done. She glanced back to Penny and then the shuttered lounge windows, which overlooked the alley at the side of the house. *Would she try to break back in that way?* Getting in through the front door would be impossible.

What about the nursery window? It was still open where she'd climbed in earlier. She delicately lifted her daughter and carried her upstairs.

Maggie reached the third step from the top and hesitated. She looked briefly down at Penny, and her eyes were half closed. Her irregular breathing had subsided but if she was going into the nursery she would grab her medication.

No activity from beyond the half closed door. Maggie gulped down her fear and ascended the last stairs. She looked left and right and then nudged inside. The window was still open, and the curtains were being gently agitated by a breeze, allowing a steady stream of snow to fall onto the carpet. She snatched up the Zyrtec from the dresser then switched off the light, swiftly closed the window and peered out at the alley. Hefty flakes were rapidly falling, and she couldn't see any movement at the drainpipe beside the pane or in the darkness below. She took a sharp pace back, in case a gun was pointed at her, then wrenched the curtains fully closed.

If she was being watched the woman now knew where she was. *Should she remain here though?* It was certainly the best option if her attacker was on ground level. She could keep her gun trained on the door and still use the drainpipe if she had to escape.

She scrambled to her bedroom and lay Penny on the bed. If she had to go outside she needed to get dressed. Watching the door and listening for signs of movement downstairs she hastily pulled on a pair of jeans, a thick black turtleneck, and her green puffer jacket before sliding her feet into some boots and zipping them tightly up her legs. She grabbed her cell and car key from the nightstand and slid them into her front pocket along with the Zyrtec. Then she hunted out the extra bullets for the gun in the drawer and reloaded.

No sounds from within the house. She transferred Penny back to the nursery and put her carefully in her crib. The room was freezing, so she found an extra blanket and draped it over her before pushing the door shut and locking them inside.

It was pitch-black. Maggie waited, revolver clutched in her hand, her breaths shallow and her legs wobbling on the heels of her boots.

CHAPTER TWENTY-TWO

Holly was crouching behind the ivy-clad, shoulder-height boundary wall beside Maggie's house that partitioned the row from McHerry Street. There was no traffic and only a few cars parked up the other side of it. She shakily applied the adhesive dressing to her wound. Pulling her T-shirt, pullover, and poncho back over it she shivered, but her scalp still felt hot and itchy in her woollen hat. She glimpsed her watch.

12:02 a.m.

Just under seven hours until sunrise.

She'd heard the nursery window closing and stared up at the sealed curtains. *Was she still in there?* She couldn't spot the drone in the charcoal sky behind the snowfall, but knew it was monitoring her next move. *Where was Babysitter?* She didn't know anything about the range of drones. *Was he seated in a car nearby, or watching in comfort from miles away?*

There was nobody else in Bozeman Street. Houses on both sides were lit by a row of spherical streetlights and only a couple of large windows were illuminated in the top rooms of a house at the far left end. The cold air was slowly reviving her, or was it the painkillers working? Gripping the flower head hard in her palm she focussed on two inescapable facts: Babysitter knew her every move; Babysitter wouldn't return Abigail until Maggie was dead.

There was no leverage. And time was running out.

She had to think only of Abigail. Contemplate the image she'd been blocking of her daughter in a stranger's arms. Use it as the worst kind of incentive to see the night out. She took a few more breaths and ignored the low-key twinge of the wound at her waist. She slid the flower head into her right sleeve and tentatively limped back towards the house. Staying in the shadow of the wall, Holly didn't take her eyes from the upstairs windows. All dark. *Was Maggie watching her approach?*

She'd had an idea and needed to get back to the rear of the property while Maggie was upstairs. She couldn't afford to let her guard down though. As she stepped back into the alley she slid the knife out of her pocket with one hand, kept her Browning raised in the other and trod the snow as lightly as she could. Her gut trembled as well as her jaw.

Weak light still glowed behind the shuttered windows and spilled out of the kitchen onto the yard. She glanced in. Didn't look like Maggie had unbolted the inner door.

Holly took out the keys and quietly unlocked the back door again. She opened it and cautiously stepped back inside the kitchen, the warmth of the room melting the flakes on her eyelashes and face. Blinking away the moisture she stole to the cupboard under the sink. She placed the knife on the drainer, silently tugged the doors and tried to suppress a hiss of pain as she knelt to look inside.

Behind the box of paintbrushes and rollers she found something she could use. It was a tube of barbecue lighter gel.

Gingerly searching through the kitchen drawers she found a box of matches in the third one down. The contents rattled as she shook them. Without hesitating, Holly knelt at the bolted door and squirted the creamy contents of the tube along the bottom of the panel and then further up the wood. Hopefully the smoke would seep under the door, and Maggie would smell it and get out before Penny was in any real danger.

She looked to the ceiling and found a smoke alarm. Holly hoped there were others in the house. She would leave via the back door and lock it again. Unless Maggie had a spare key, she would have to escape through the front, and that's where Holly would be waiting for her.

Holly listened at the door for movement in the lounge and then took a match out of the box and struck it. She gulped as the flame burst and flickered and held it an inch from the wood.

Holding her breath, she touched it to the door. Nothing happened. She played the flame over the white pools but they only sizzled and browned. Returning to the cupboard she located a bottle of spirit amongst the paintbrushes.

When she got back to the door there was a tiny flame weakly licking at it. Holly squirted the spirit over it, and the flame surged outwards before rolling up. Black patches appeared on the panel behind the shimmering yellow, and Holly stood back and watched the veneer begin to bubble. There was a lot of smoke, and that was exactly what she wanted.

But the flames enlarged quickly until the door was entirely covered by them, and she had to stand back from the heat and cover her mouth. The smoke alarm began to squeal above her. She could also hear one in the lounge, sounding just out of sync with the first.

Maggie would already be looking for an exit, so Holly reversed back out of the door and pulled it shut behind her. She watched the smoke waft against the glass as she locked it and felt a stab of guilt about sealing Maggie and her child inside. But Maggie could get out the front or break a window, and Holly had to be ready for every eventuality. And there was something much more significant to consider when she did emerge.

Holly gazed up at the window above her. No light on. Gripping the Browning tight she scuttled back down the alleyway. The snow was falling so hard now she couldn't even see the end of it. Shit. She'd left the knife on the drainer. No time to go back. *If Maggie were heading for the front door how fast would she get there? Surely she wouldn't attempt to enter the kitchen.*

Holly kept low as she reached the windows again and dashed back onto the street. She crouched and waited behind the cover of the wall, gun pointing at the front door and eyes flitting between the panes.

If the door opened she would tell Maggie to lay Penny down. If she didn't immediately comply she would threaten to open fire. Maggie would have to obey. She would assure her that she would take care of Penny. And then she'd have to pull the trigger. Pull it a couple of times. She couldn't hesitate. Holly had to consider what it would mean for Abigail if she did that again.

She didn't look up but knew the drone would be swooping there, relaying the moment the two women came properly face-to-face.

CHAPTER TWENTY-THREE

Holly was convinced five minutes had passed, and still there was no sign of Maggie. Her hands shook as she held the gun on the front door. She could now see the smoke curling around the edges of the curtains in the darkened nursery window. In her ears the alarms had become one tone.

Maggie would be calculating her best way out. She couldn't get out via the kitchen; it had to be an inferno in there by now. Holly could see the dull light from the side windows in the alley and would spot any attempt to leave via those.

She scanned the other nine houses in the left row. Somebody would raise the alarm soon, and she prayed the fire wouldn't spread to the other homes.

If nobody else had, she'd call the emergency services as soon as... *as soon as what? She'd murdered Maggie?* Holly didn't even know what would happen when she discharged the brand new weapon. Guns kicked and she could still miss. That's if she really could pull the trigger on another human being. She couldn't even swallow.

A loud crash. Glass breaking. From behind the house.

Perhaps Maggie had spotted her waiting in the shadows, and this was a ploy to lure Holly to the yard so she could make a run for it through the front. Holly stayed rooted to the spot. Maggie couldn't stay inside with Penny much longer.

She counted to thirty. No other commotion from the rear. Had she already climbed down with Penny and was already fleeing through the yard? It bordered woods so once she'd made it there she could lose herself, and it would be impossible for Holly to locate her in the dark.

Using the back of her hand to quickly wipe the snow from her face she left the cover of the wall. Stealthily trotting down the alley, Holly pointed her Browning at each window and found them all filled with smoke. A grey cloud billowed at her from the direction of the kitchen, and she crouched and aimed her weapon ahead as the fumes bit her eyes. There was a caustic smell of burning plastic, and she clamped her mouth shut and tried not to breathe in through her nose.

A sharp crack from behind her.

Holly spun, expecting to find Maggie standing there with her weapon raised. But as she swung the gun around the alley her eyes were watering and she could hardly see.

She covered her mouth with her free palm and squinted back the way she'd come. A stream of smoke was escaping from one of the lounge windows through a fissure in the top right corner. The heat was about to explode it from its frame.

Holly turned and ran on through the smoke to the yard. She had to get oxygen before she passed out. But there was little to be found when she rounded the corner.

The kitchen pane was blackened but intact; but when Holly looked up at the window above it she could see it was shattered and two knotted sheets were dangling down like a rope.

Holly swivelled to the yard, but through the blizzard, could scarcely see a few feet ahead. She stepped forward and took a few breaths of cool air and was about to cross the lawn when she stopped herself and examined the ground. The snow was deep, but there wasn't a single footprint.

She headed back down the alley. It had been a decoy and, in the brief time she'd gone to investigate the breaking window, Maggie had probably slipped out with Penny.

When she reached the front of the house she expected the door to be ajar. But it was still sealed. Holly blinked and squinted at McHerry Street. No sign of her there or any sound of receding footsteps, but it was difficult to hear properly under the din of the alarms and the boom of the flames inside the house.

She pushed on the wooden door. Locked. *Could Maggie be waiting behind it?* She took a pace back, and her eyes shot to a light as it came on in the upstairs of a house three doors along. Looked like the alarms were stirring people awake. *Where the hell had Maggie gone?*

CHAPTER TWENTY-FOUR

'Which service?'

'I want to report a fire at 1 Bozeman Street, Whitsun.' Holly stayed behind the cover of the ivy-clad boundary wall as her eyes combed the street for a sign of Maggie.

'Can I get some details?' the female operator asked.

'Just get here as—'

A loud crack. Sounded like a gun discharging. Holly waited for the pain.

'Ma'am?'

An SUV was parked outside a house two doors along from Maggie's, and in the streetlight she could see there was something silver lying on the hood. She swung back to McHerry, but there was still nobody there.

'Ma'am?'

Holly hung up and pocketed the phone. The Browning felt slippery in her grip as she pointed it at the SUV. *Was that?* Cautiously she approached and confirmed it was a revolver. She grabbed it and tucked it in her left poncho pocket before her eyes darted to the roof above. All the houses in the row were joined. She stepped backwards and craned her neck and could see an attic window in Maggie's roof. It was open. Sticking close to the front doors she limped towards the dead end of the row.

'Who are you?'

Holly turned back to find a middle-aged, redheaded man in tight-fitting black pyjamas half cowering behind his door.

'There's a fire.' Holly nodded at Maggie's home and kept her weapon hidden behind her leg.

He didn't appear to believe her and took off his spectacles. 'You're not a resident.'

'That house is burning down.' She nodded again. 'You should call the emergency services.' She had to get him back inside.

He peered down the row and gasped: 'Jesus wept.' He fixed her accusingly. 'Where have you come from?'

'I was just passing by.'

His brow hardened. 'At this time?'

'Better call them. It's spreading fast.'

He seemed in two minds about whether to leave her, but then disappeared back inside, yelling: 'Jean!' A dog started barking.

Holly made her way to the last house. She rounded the corner and found a fire escape at the side. There was nobody on it. She reversed a few feet to see if there was any movement above. *Was Maggie still on the roof?* She squinted into the shadows of the yard behind her but it was empty. Maybe she'd heard Holly's conversation with the neighbour and was staying up there until she thought she'd gone. She could hear the man who had just stopped her. He was talking on his phone in the street.

'I want to report a fire in Bozeman Street… On their way now?'

If she hung around he was probably going to attempt a citizen's arrest. *Should she start climbing?* Maggie would have nowhere to go. And now she was unarmed. She put one foot on the bottom step, gripped the cold metal handrail and kept her eyes on the top of the escape.

'Maggie? Are you both OK?' The neighbour's voice echoed.

Holly halted and headed back into the row. Maggie was in front of the houses on the opposite side clutching Penny in a blanket and was almost to the end of the street. She must have come down the escape and slipped by her while she had the exchange with the neighbour. 'Stop!'

Maggie turned, and so did he.

'We're going to wait for the police to arrive.' He held up a hand. 'Think you should wait with us.'

Holly extended the gun as she falteringly approached.

At first the neighbour didn't react, but then he saw what she had in her hand. His arms immediately rose, and his combative expression drained away. 'Whoa.'

'Go back inside and close the door.'

Another front door opened nearby and an elderly man in an orange robe emerged.

'Go back inside!'

He immediately obeyed Holly, and the first neighbour complied as well.

Maggie didn't move except to swing Penny to the far side of her so she was shielded from Holly.

Holly slowed about six feet from her. 'Put her down.' She moved forward another pace so she could see her through the snow. This was it. It was Maggie or Abigail.

'We can work this out. He doesn't need to know.'

Holly shook her head. 'He's watching us now, up there. He's got a drone buzzing around.'

Maggie briefly raised her eyes, but dropped them back to Holly as if it might be a trick.

Holly tensed her body and could see Maggie was desperately trying to figure a way out of the situation. 'I've got your gun. I don't want to shoot with Penny in your arms, but if you move now I'll pull this trigger.'

'Ever fired one of those before?'

Holly didn't respond.

Don't listen to her.

'No, you haven't. You're scared out of your wits, and I don't blame you.'

'Stop talking.' Holly's heart pounded at the back of her brain.

'Maybe you should call Babysitter.'

'I said stop talking.' Holly focussed on her chin.

'If you do it, you're going straight to jail.'

'It didn't stop you.' Holly clenched her jaw.

'That was just you and me. If he sees exactly what's going on here he'll know there'll be too many witnesses. We can offer to cover for him. Tell him we'll square things with the police. If we stay silent, maybe he'll spare both our children.'

Holly could see Maggie was going to use any argument to stay alive for Penny. This was her last opportunity to do what Babysitter demanded. 'Lay Penny on the floor now,' she whispered.

Maggie didn't.

Don't think about it. Just do it.

'Think of Penny. I'm counting three. Whatever you choose to do before that is up to you. One… two…'

CHAPTER TWENTY-FIVE

Maggie contemplated the woman's finger tighten on the trigger. *Had she underestimated her?* She cursed; after tucking the snubbie in the waistband of her jeans to make her way across the roof with Penny she'd watched it clatter and slide off it before she could react.

'The police are on their way!'

Her neighbour, Chuck Bretton, was disobeying his order to stay inside and hiding himself behind the front door to shout through the gap.

'Put the gun down!'

'Listen to him.' Maggie twisted her body so Penny was entirely blocked by it. *How else could she appeal to her maternal instincts?* 'My daughter hasn't said her first word yet. Or started walking. You really gonna take those moments away from me?'

'Three.' The woman's face shifted through every conflicted emotion. A harsh wind slanted the snow across her but she remained rigid.

Maggie half closed her eyes and focussed on the barrel that was pointing straight at her chest. 'Listen to me. This situation isn't going to end well for either of us. I'll be dead, and you'll be arrested. What good will that do Abigail or Penny?'

But the woman didn't appear to hear her. Her features were blank, as if she'd emptied herself out to see through her cold-blooded task.

'Listen to me!' she screamed, hoping to snap her out of it.

Another window broke in Maggie's home.

'The situation has changed. We should both walk out of here now. I give you my word, I won't try anything. We can contact him. Ask him what we should do next.'

'I can't trust you. This is my only option,' the woman's voice sounded distant.

'Don't do it!' Chuck yelled.

Sirens. Fast approaching.

Maggie braced herself. Maybe the bullet wouldn't kill her outright. If she could, she would run at the woman and try to wrestle the gun from her before she got a second shot off.

But she still hadn't fired, and Maggie knew she had to exploit her second of indecision. 'We can play for time. My car is parked out in the street. Let's go now before we *can't* leave.'

The woman's shoulders rose as she filled her chest.

'You can keep the gun on me. I'll drive. But neither of us want to be talking to the police.'

The echo of the sirens changed as they neared Bozeman Street.

'They're here!' Chuck cried.

Maggie could feel Penny fighting the blanket. *Was it the last time she'd hold her?* Her gaze locked on the barrel.

Six seconds passed. It felt like Maggie's heart would burst.

The woman suddenly breathed out and nodded once. 'OK. OK, move.'

Maggie remained frozen.

'Go!'

A trick? She slowly turned her back. *Was this so the woman didn't have to see her expression when she fired?* She hugged Penny to her and began heading to McHerry. After a few paces she was relieved to hear footsteps crunching behind her and allowed herself to exhale.

'Try to escape and you'll leave me no choice.'

Maggie nodded emphatically as they cut through the snow and smoke. Reaching the end of the row she crossed the street to where her red Scion was parked. To her left she could see a phalanx of distant red and blues approaching from town.

'Quickly.' The woman was closer to her now.

Maggie fumbled out her key with her free hand, and the car chirped once and unlocked. 'I need to belt her in.'

'Hurry.'

Maggie opened the back door and unwrapped Penny to put her in the baby seat. She swiftly fumbled with the straps and secured her. It was pointless playing for time. She didn't want to submit to any questions either. Maggie tugged the driver's door.

Her captor circled around the car and got in the passenger's side.

Maggie pulled the door after her and started the engine. She switched on the wipers, and they sliced away the snow that had stuck to the window.

The woman kept the gun on her but peered through the windshield as the emergency vehicles slowed to make a right into Bozeman. 'What are you waiting for?'

Maggie arced in the street just before the response team disappeared into a swell of smoke and then accelerated the Scion away.

'Careful!'

The car skewed as the back wheels fought for purchase on the snow, but Maggie brought it back under control. Neither of them spoke as they quickly put distance between them and the blaze. In the rear-view Maggie could see the smoke puffing into the black sky.

'Slow down.' Her captor now had her weapon pointed at Maggie's cheek, but her attention was fixed on the road ahead.

A patrol car was fast approaching, lights flickering.

Maggie decelerated, the woman lowered the gun, and they both waited for the car to reach them. It zipped past, and Maggie watched it swerve into Bozeman before picking up speed again.

'Get us off the main road as soon as possible.'

Maggie detected the tremor in her voice. If she was as fraught as she'd been when Babysitter had taken Penny she knew what she was capable of. 'I've got both my hands on the wheel. Can you point that thing away from me?'

'Keep your eyes on the road.'

'At least tell me your name.'

'Shut up,' the woman thrust the barrel against Maggie's temple.

'Look, we'll each do whatever it takes to keep our child safe, so the best thing we can do is work this out together.'

'I said shut up. I'm the one who's already been shot, remember?'

Penny started fussing in the back seat.

'She'll be OK.' The gun shook in the woman's hand. 'Just put your foot down.'

CHAPTER TWENTY-SIX

Holly knew she'd missed her chance. She should have pulled the trigger. She'd been so close, had almost bypassed herself and managed to exert enough pressure to fulfil the task. But she couldn't have fired on Maggie while she still held Penny. And Maggie was right; with witnesses to the execution the police would have soon captured her. Surely that wasn't what Babysitter wanted.

'It's OK, ssshhh.' Maggie soothed Penny.

Penny grumbled a little but seemed reassured by her mother's presence.

Holly knew it was dangerous to become part of Maggie's game plan. She'd already got Penny back. She had much less to lose. If Holly were Maggie she'd try to escape as soon as possible. But, for the moment, it made sense for them both to run and stay out of the police's way until they'd agreed on a story to tell them. And they could contact Babysitter to see if that was something they could bargain with. But she already suspected what his response would be.

She tugged off her black wool watch cap, and Maggie glanced briefly at her flattened auburn curls.

'Eyes front,' Holly barked. The air cooled her hot scalp but made her feel dizzy. *The painkillers?* She looked beyond the snow swirling in front of the headlights to the blackness ahead. Maggie was driving them into the country, and the streetlights were already becoming further spaced out. She gazed briefly upwards. *Was the drone still overhead or were they now out of its range?* If Babysitter had been watching what had just happened it would have appeared that Holly had taken Maggie hostage. Not that it had been Maggie's suggestion. As far as he was concerned Holly could be relocating her in order to carry out his instructions.

That was still an option. But maybe that was the last thing he wanted if it meant Holly's arrest and interrogation might compromise his possible role in the murders in East County. 'I'm going to contact him now.' She struggled her phone out of her pocket while she kept the barrel firmly on Maggie. 'Don't take your hands off the wheel.'

Maggie nodded. 'I'm not going to do anything to endanger Penny.'

Holly believed her. Even though her child was strapped in she didn't think she'd attempt to escape while they were doing sixty. Not until she'd heard the outcome of her dialogue with Babysitter anyway.

Several witnesses now involved. Have taken Maggie prisoner. Please advise.

Holly sent the message.

'What did you say to him?'

Holly wiped the cold sheen off her face but didn't answer.

'Come on. This is going to take both of us to work out who the hell he is and why he's doing this to us.'

But Holly didn't want to give Maggie even the vague notion she was about to buddy up and wouldn't use the gun. 'Pick up your speed. Once they speak to your neighbour they'll be coming straight after us.'

Maggie puffed the snow off her fringe. 'We should head into West Acre.'

'What's that?'

'Nature reserve. Means we can get off this road.'

'OK.' Holly was already suspicious. 'Where is it?'

'Just coming to it.'

*

They drove in silence until the sign came into view.

Holly studied the image of a happy family having a picnic by a pond. 'Won't it be closed?'

'The aviary will be but you can drive through the forest any time.'

'Let's do it then.'

Maggie made a right, and they hit a narrow gravel path bordered by potted trees.

Holly briefly checked on Penny. Her eyes were open, and she seemed happy enough. *Where was Abigail now? Had she endangered her even more by not pulling the trigger?* 'What's on the other side of the forest?'

'Riverton. Just farms and a few houses but the forest will take us at least half an hour to clear.'

'Don't slow down then.'

The car juddered as it dropped into a dry ford and then went back up a steep slope. The ticket booth for the aviary appeared under overhanging branches but Maggie took a left fork and they followed a more uneven track that wound its way around the larger trees of the forest.

Holly's phone vibrated, and she opened the message that had arrived from Babysitter.

Too cosy for you in the house, Holly? Must be getting awkward in that car. Change of plan. Just get yourself as far away from having to answer any questions as possible. New instructions soon.

'What does he say?' Maggie asked warily, when she knew Holly had had enough time to read it.

'Looks like he's reconsidering.'

'OK – what did he say specifically?' She clearly didn't believe her.

Holly figured it was better to placate her so she wouldn't try anything as soon as she got a chance. 'Take a look.' She held out the message for her.

Maggie squinted at it.

'You wear specs normally?'

Maggie nodded. 'I left them at the house. Didn't have much time to remember them,' she added caustically.

They were back on the straight for a while and then came to a short wooden bridge. The car rumbled over it.

Holly grunted as it juddered her wound.

'So your name's Holly.'

Holly realised Maggie had just seen it in Babysitter's message.

'Holly what?'

'Just Holly.'

'Come on. You know everything about me.'

Holly raised the Browning again.

'What?'

'Credit me with some intelligence.'

'What did Babysitter tell you I'd done?'

Holly frowned, but knew exactly what Maggie was talking about.

'That's how he makes it easier. He told me something about Janet Braun to make me believe she was less than human.'

Holly didn't reply.

'Tell me your surname.'

'Don't ask that again.'

Maggie doubled the speed of the wipers. Even under the trees the snow was falling thickly. 'Don't believe what he told you. I knew it was a lie when I broke into Janet's home. But I needed to believe it. I couldn't have done it otherwise.'

'But you didn't go through with it.'

Maggie kept her attention on the road. 'No.' She nodded, as if convincing herself.

Holly still doubted Babysitter would have given Penny back to her if she'd let Janet Braun live. But she hadn't heard the name on the news. *Was the body still waiting to be discovered?* But if things had got out of hand as they had tonight it was a hope she could still cling to. 'Tell me the truth about Janet Braun.'

'I have.' Maggie didn't blink.

Holly shook her head, and the car continued to swerve them from side to side while the wipers chopped at the screen.

She glimpsed at her watch.

12:31 a.m.

Less than six and a half hours until sunrise.

Penny gurgled in the back, and Holly resisted the temptation to turn and check on her again. She hoped that Abigail was sleeping, that she didn't even know her mother wasn't nearby.

Her phone buzzed. Instructions had arrived.

CHAPTER TWENTY-SEVEN

Maggie tried to gauge Holly's reaction after she'd read the new message from Babysitter, but her face was impassive. 'Well?'

'He's sent an address. Said we should make our way there as quickly as we can.'

'And?'

'That's it.'

Maggie didn't believe her.

Holly read out the zip code. 'I'll put it in the satnav.' She entered it.

Was that all that had been in the text? She doubted it because otherwise Holly would have shown it to her. But Maggie didn't want to aggravate her captor. Not with her holding both firearms and Penny in the back of the car. From their exchange in the street she knew how close Holly had come to taking her life and realised she had to make that decision as difficult for her as she could. Maggie decided to be as compliant as possible.

Hard flakes fizzed on the roof as they passed through an open area of the forest. Both of them waited.

Holly leaned forward to study the map. 'It's in Astley, eighteen miles from here. We'll have to circle back on ourselves after we've cleared the forest but I think we should keep going this way until we're sure we've lost the police.'

Maggie nodded and darted her eyes to the screen. The route took them into the heart of Astley. It was the nearest big town, and she'd had Penny in its main hospital.

'Just get us there. You don't have your child to shield you now, so don't think I won't shoot you. You didn't have any problems pulling the trigger on me.'

'Can I at least drop Penny with a friend to look after?'

'No,' Holly said flatly.

But she'd paused before replying, and Maggie suspected she was thinking about it. 'I promise I won't try anything, and I'll come with you anywhere you want. Penny needs to be changed and fed.'

'She'll be fine. At least she can be with you.' Holly fought to keep the tremor out of her voice.

Maggie felt for her. The fear for her daughter's life had almost debilitated her every time she thought of Penny in the clutches of Babysitter. But the only motive Holly could have for exposing Penny to further danger was so she could make sure Maggie remained obedient. 'Surely you don't want to risk her life. She's been through all that already.'

'You're in no position to make demands—'

'I'm not. But if I know Penny's in a safe place then you can be assured that I'll cooperate.'

'You have to anyway. Concentrate on not wrapping us around a tree.'

'I have a friend in Astley. I could drop Penny there.'

'I've said no. I don't want to delay our getting to this address one second longer than I have to.'

'But it will only take a minute.' But Maggie knew she was already pushing it too far.

'Don't ask again.'

Maggie wouldn't but she'd planted the seed. If Holly thought about it she'd see it made sense. It certainly meant that Holly wouldn't have to take responsibility for Penny if she did follow through with her orders.

The car dropped down into a darker area where the snow hadn't yet penetrated.

'Where in Astley does your friend live?' Holly was studying the screen again.

'Brentwood. It's on the outskirts.'

'I know it. Specific address?'

'Prospect Drive.'

Holly just nodded. *Was she considering leaving her daughter there, or had she asked because she wanted to know where she could take Penny after she'd killed Maggie?*

'Babysitter told me Janet Braun was involved in distributing child porn. What have you been told about me, Holly?'

'Stop talking.'

'And what do you think the woman who comes to kill you is going to be told?'

Holly flinched and readjusted her position in the seat.

'If you kill me you might get Abigail back, but then, a few days from now, somebody like you is going to come visit. You'll be ready for them, but you'll have to live with the idea that someone else will take their place. And unless you can stop them Penny *and* Abigail will be without their mothers.'

'I'm just thinking about Abigail right now.'

That's what Maggie had to fear most. 'And we have no idea where we're driving to. Maybe Babysitter is the Slayer and he's setting a trap before we can speak to the cops.'

A low branch scraped across the roof of the car.

Holly gestured with the barrel of the gun for Maggie to keep her eyes on the road. 'What other choice is there?'

'We have to stop this now. If we walk in there it's over for us… and our daughters.'

CHAPTER TWENTY-EIGHT

Whatever her motives, Holly knew she couldn't ignore what Maggie had said. Babysitter would want to silence both of them. 'I'm not jeopardising Abigail. We drive to the address and check it out before we go in there.'

'Maybe it'll be too late by then. Perhaps he's planning to ambush us before we even reach it.' Maggie scrutinized Penny in the mirror.

'She's fine. And how could he do that?'

'He knows we'll have this conversation. He's going to be trying to think one step ahead of us. He doesn't know how far we are away from Astley though.'

'So what edge does that give us?' Maggie had a point: *what would happen to Abigail if he did attack both of them in Astley?*

'We have to think about this. Let me pull over.'

'Keep driving,' Holly snapped. 'And grip the wheel with both hands.' She couldn't allow Maggie to call any of the shots. 'I don't want Abigail to spend one more second away from me than she has to.' She leaned on her right side to take the weight off her wound.

'I understand that. But obeying him isn't going to guarantee you getting her back.'

'It did for you,' Holly said stolidly.

Maggie squinted at the road, as if wanting to focus anywhere but on responding.

'Sorry, I forgot. You got lucky at Janet's house. But if there were a chance you'd guess Babysitter was the East County Slayer why did he let you walk away?'

'He didn't. You came calling. And, like I say, once you've taken care of me it'll probably be your turn. But with the police in pursuit he can't afford to have us around for long.'

Holly kept her eyes on the older woman's expression. 'Babysitter told me you were a killer who had escaped justice.'

Maggie nodded. 'And when you did your online research, as I did with Janet, what did you find?'

Holly's body slanted left as they negotiated another bend and the wound flared against the sudden pressure. 'Nothing.' She grunted as her stomach muscles clenched.

'But you still want to believe it, don't you? I had to believe it of Janet although she was probably just a struggling mother like us.'

'Was?'

'Jesus, stop trying to trip me up. I don't know why Babysitter targeted us. I spend my days processing dental health insurance claims. Penny is my only slice of happiness.'

'I know all that.'

'And I guess you're the same.'

Holly wouldn't be drawn. But Maggie wasn't far off base. After paying for childcare, the hours she spent as a clerk in the offices of a small, family-owned law firm barely paid the bills. But Abigail made every day worth it. 'So why the hell is Babysitter doing this?'

'Maybe we can figure that out.'

Holly registered Maggie was using the word 'we' again. But even though a part of her wanted to share the torture of what Babysitter was putting them through she couldn't trust her. 'What if he does know exactly where we are?'

'The drone?' Maggie said sceptically.

'I saw it.' But Holly could see she was unconvinced. 'And what about this?' She held up her phone. 'Could he be tracking it?'

'If he does, he'll know the exact moment we get into Astley.'

'So there's no edge.' The meds were relieving the pain in Holly's hip; but as she squeezed her pullover sleeve and made sure the dried flower head was still where she tucked it a new thought occurred to her.

Maggie glimpsed at the satnav. 'So what are our options? Either we go there or we don't.'

'There is another alternative.'

'What?'

'You go there alone.'

Maggie glared at her. 'Why the hell would I do that?'

'Because it's what you'll have to agree to if you want me to make sure Penny is in a safe place.' Holly watched the muscle pulse at the side of her jaw.

'He's not going to let me go.'

'If you're right, he needs to silence both of us. You negotiate with him.'

'Don't be naïve. Even if it does work we'll both be looking over our shoulders.'

'I know. Which is why I'll follow him afterwards. If we can find out who he is then he has no power.'

Maggie's pupils darted. '*If* you can follow him. That's a real long shot.'

'We could build a file. Tell him to stop and that that will buy our silence.' But Holly doubted it would be as straightforward as that.

'And ensure it's released to the police if anything should happen to us?'

'Exactly.'

Maggie chewed her lip, as if considering it.

But Holly was positive Maggie was planning on something before they even got to Astley.

CHAPTER TWENTY-NINE

Maggie swerved around another bend, and the Scion thudded into a hole in the road.

Holly winced as the car bounced.

'You'll let me drop Penny off with my friend first?' She had to convince Holly she'd go along with her proposition.

'As long as you don't try anything. If there's a sign of that it'll be the last time I trust you and the last time I hesitate to use this.' Holly brandished the Browning as if Maggie needed reminding of its presence.

'OK. What if I don't come out of my meeting with Babysitter?' Maggie wanted to give her plenty to think about.

'That's my problem.'

'Then you've got to promise me you'll return to my friend and make sure she understands Penny has become her responsibility.'

'She must be a good friend.'

Maggie nodded. She wasn't about to tell her it was her younger sister, Sascha. 'I need your word as a mother on that.'

'I promise,' Holly said solemnly.

'Then my only other condition is that you let me out to pee.'

'How dumb do you think I am?'

Maggie decelerated.

'What are you doing? Put your foot back down.'

'What are you gonna make me do, go all over the seat? My bladder's about to burst.'

'Keep driving!' Holly ordered.

But Maggie was pulling them over to the side of the road. 'You'll have Penny here with you. I'll do it in front of the headlights. I have to.' She opened the door.

'Stay in the car!'

Maggie scuttled ten feet in front of the vehicle and dropped her jeans to her ankles with her back to it. There was no gunshot. No sign of Holly getting out. If she had any sense she'd stay with Penny.

She started peeing, and sighed a few times for effect. The snow on the illuminated road glistened and flakes landed cold on her scalp.

She leaned forward in her squatting position and deftly slid her hand into the right front pocket of her jeans and plucked out her phone. She had to use it before Holly found it on her. The urine steamed between her knees but she was nearly done. She grunted and sighed loudly.

'Hurry up!' Holly yelled.

But Maggie knew she had no choice but to wait. She was positive that Holly had another agenda but right now there was nothing she could do. Holly needed Maggie, and however real her threats were she knew she wouldn't harm Penny.

She hastily sent a text and slid the phone back into her pocket before standing and hitching up her jeans. She swivelled and trotted back to the Scion. 'I'm sorry. I had no control over that.'

'Get back in the car.' Holly was aiming the gun at her through the open door.

Maggie checked on Penny, saw she was asleep and climbed back into the driver's seat. She didn't turn to look at Holly's expression.

Holly's breath squealed through her nose. 'Drive.'

Maggie pulled the door shut, put on her seat belt and accelerated down the forest road. The barrel of the gun was shoved into her right ear.

'Don't hold us up again or Penny will be staying where she is.'

'I'm sorry. I was in pain.'

'I don't care about your pain. Only my daughter.'

CHAPTER THIRTY

Holly kept the gun firmly on Maggie. The trees gradually thinned out, and the harsh blizzard crackled around the car as they motored through the vortex of snow ahead.

'Next left,' the male satnav voice instructed them.

They hit the highway and twenty minutes later were making a right and passing the sign to Astley.

Holly checked the dash.

1:15 a.m.

Under six hours until sunrise. 'So your friend lives in Brentwood.' Holly knew the neighbourhood. It was on the wealthier side of town.

'Yes.' Maggie was examining the satnav. 'I can be in and out in minutes.'

'But if Babysitter is tracking us he'll know exactly where we've gone.' She observed Maggie blink rapidly as if considering the dilemma.

'We could park up on the edge of the neighbourhood and walk the last few blocks.'

But Holly had already pre-empted the suggestion. 'Just get us there as quickly as possible.'

Traffic was sparse but there were a couple of snow tractors already in service in the tree-lined suburbs. Astley was a fishing town that didn't cater for tourists but had a lively scene for its inhabitants if you knew where to find it. Holly had had fun waitressing there when she'd been in college, but hadn't returned since.

The car threaded its way through the winding road to the wharf but then Maggie turned them left towards the conspicuously modern housing development bolted to the hills above it.

'Prospect Drive, up ahead' Maggie slowed the Scion. 'We can walk the rest of the way.' She'd halted at the bottom of someone's steep drive.

'How far is it from here?'

'About two hundred yards, street on the left.'

'Number?'

Maggie seemed to know what was coming next and said nothing.

'I'm the only one who's going.'

'No way. You're not taking Penny.'

'You know I'll take good care of her,' Holly reassured her.

Maggie shook her head.

'I can't trust you out of my sight. You'll get into the trunk, and I'll lock it so you can't follow.'

'So you can come back and put a bullet in me.' She glanced down at the Browning in Holly's hand.

'In a residential street? I'll drop Penny with your friend and come back and let you out. Then we both go to the address. I still need you to talk to Babysitter. I can't risk Abigail being left defenceless if I go in there alone.' But Holly could see Maggie wasn't convinced. 'Come on, we're losing time. This is the only way I'm going with this or we take off now and Penny comes with us.'

Maggie didn't budge.

'Wait there. I'll fetch her from the back and you can have a moment with her.'

Holly got out of the passenger side before Maggie could respond. She ignored the harsh breeze and flakes blasting her face, tugged the rear door behind Maggie and unlocked the belt securing Penny in her chair. She was still sleeping. 'Come on now.' Gingerly lifting her out, Holly wrapped her in the blanket, closed the back door with her foot and held her out to Maggie's window.

Maggie opened her door, took her and hugged her so her face rested in the crook of her neck. She regarded the Browning. 'I'll be coming back,' she whispered against Penny's ear. 'I'll be coming back real soon.'

'OK. Let me take her.'

Maggie was reluctant to let go.

'Come on. Or you can drive the three of us.' But Holly found it impossible not to empathise with the moment.

Maggie briefly closed her eyes, kissed the crown of her daughter's head and gave her back to Holly.

Holly carefully cradled Penny. 'What's your friend's name?'

'Sascha.'

'OK. Number?'

'It's 335.'

'Round to the back.'

Maggie slowly emerged and closed the driver's door.

'In the trunk.'

She folded her arms.

'Come on. If I was going to shoot you I could do it now.' She looked up and down the streetlit road but there was nobody about. 'Open the trunk and get in.'

Maggie regarded her child in Holly's arms. 'Hold her tightly. Shield her from the cold.'

Holly nodded, but didn't move from the spot.

The wind pulled at Maggie's hair.

'Go on.' Holly gestured at the trunk.

Maggie didn't take her gaze from Penny as she lifted the lid. 'See you soon.' Then she climbed inside.

Holly trotted around and slammed it in place, briefly relieved that Maggie was incapable while she was dealing with Penny. *Should she leave her in there even after she'd returned?* It was worth considering. She didn't want any surprises for the remainder of the journey. 'I'll be right back,' she whispered at the trunk and checked she wasn't being watched through any of the surrounding windows. But they were all curtained and in darkness.

Holly hobbled to 335 with Penny clutched to her shoulder.

CHAPTER THIRTY-ONE

Penny breathed into Holly's ear. 'Ssshhh.' She could already feel her tense and the distress starting to build inside her tiny form. Penny knew her mother was getting further away, and Holly felt torn up by separating them. 'It's all right.' Holly snuggled her closer to protect her from the chill wind and the icy crystals blowing against them. She inhaled her fragrant skin. Penny smelt so good, and her desperation to embrace her own daughter tightened her throat.

Even though it had been Maggie's idea, getting her out of harm's way was the right thing to do. Holly wouldn't endanger a child, and both mothers knew it. It would give them peace of mind and, without the distraction, they could focus on their appointment with Babysitter.

Holly had weakened her position. With Penny in safe hands all Maggie had to do was escape. But if she kept her in the trunk then held the gun on her when they arrived at the address she would have no choice but to comply. But Holly had to be on her guard.

Penny emitted a gurgle of discomfort.

'I know it's cold. We'll soon be there.' Holly tuned out the prickle of her wound. 'Then you can have some milk. Would you like that?'

Penny's hand emerged from her blanket and touched Holly's face. It was hot, and her fingers clutched at her chin.

Holly turned left onto Prospect, followed the line of glowing, ornate streetlights and took in the mock, shingle-style homes with their gambrel roofs and extensive porches. It looked like Maggie had some wealthy friends. It was a long street, and she had to cover some ground before she found 335.

Penny squirmed in her arms.

'It's all right. We're nearly there.' She limped faster and crossed over to the right side.

Number 335 was the only house with its gates open. Holly stepped onto the expansive drive and approached the front door. There were lights on in the lower windows. She'd already decided on her plan of action. She would knock, tell Sascha she was a friend of Maggie's, get her to take Penny and say she was going to help Maggie bring in Penny's things and that Maggie would explain everything. Then she'd turn and exit the street as fast as possible. The main thing was that Penny would be safe.

The blue surgical gloves would arouse suspicion so Holly stripped them off and pocketed them. The cool air burnt her fingers. Hitching Penny up higher in her left arm she pressed the doorbell with the barrel of her gun. She was about to stow the weapon, but decided to keep it hidden under her poncho. There was no way of knowing if this was who Maggie said it was.

Just hand her over, make the excuses and leave.

Something slammed into the back of her skull.

Holly stumbled against the panel and suddenly hands were gripping Penny to catch her if she fell.

'Let her go!' a female voice screamed from behind her.

Holly rounded on her and found a blonde woman in her late twenties wielding a heavy saucepan. The blow hadn't properly registered yet but her yelling was muffled. Holly had dropped the gun.

'Put her down!' The woman looked terrified.

The drive wobbled under the soles of Holly's feet as she searched the white around her boots for the Browning and extended her free right hand to ward off further attack. Maggie's gun was in her left pocket, and she'd have to put Penny down to get it.

The woman took a pace forward and brandished the saucepan, grasping the handle with both hands and swinging it to the side of her face in readiness to assault Holly again.

Holly blinked as the woman's threats barely penetrated the fizzing in her ears. A harsh impact from behind. Was there a second attacker? But she realised she'd collapsed backwards against the front door. She slid herself back up the panel, straightened her legs and protectively hugged Penny.

The woman came forward to strike her a second time, and she tried to block with her arm. The heavy-bottomed implement struck it. Holly's exclamation was locked inside her head. She lashed out and caught the woman under the chin with her fist. She retreated, shock registering more than pain.

'Give me her! I've called the police!'

Holly doubted that. *When the hell had Maggie warned the woman to expect Holly though?* Holly ran at her but, despite her petrified expression, she held her ground and swiped at her with the saucepan again.

It only caught Holly weakly on her wrist as she shielded herself, used the right side of her body to bulldoze through and made for the gate, her left arm defending Penny as she staggered over the slush.

She was sure she'd toppled her assailant, but as she hit the street Holly heard the woman on her heels.

Swivelling back she found her only a foot away, teeth bared and saucepan raised.

CHAPTER THIRTY-TWO

Maggie was curled in a foetal position in her cell. It smelt of tyre rubber and carpet and the only illumination was her phone. She'd been counting the minutes since Holly had walked away with Penny. Nineteen had passed. Had Sascha followed her instructions and subdued Holly?

Over the whisper of the snowflakes she could discern a set of footsteps approaching. Sitting up quickly in her confined space, she bashed her scalp on the lid. Maggie ignored the pain and strained her ears. They were definitely headed in her direction. Their sound changed as they crossed the road to the car.

Maggie held her breath.

A cough she recognised.

'Penny?'

'Penny's safe. No thanks to you.' It was Holly's slurred voice.

Maggie closed her eyes.

'You shouldn't have done that…'

Something thudded against the trunk.

'Holly?'

No response.

'Holly? Talk to me.'

Silence. 'Holly!' *Had she been injured and just fallen? What if she'd dropped Penny?* Maggie rapped her knuckles against the inside of the lid.

Something slid down it.

'Holly!' She banged again.

Penny started crying.

Oh Jesus. This was her fault. She should have just gone along with Holly and let her drop Penny off. But she hadn't known if Holly would try anything. 'Holly, wake up!'

Penny sobbed the other side of the sealed metal. She'd already tried the lock but fumbled with it again. 'Calm down, sweetheart, I'm here.'

But her disembodied words seemed to make her daughter even more upset.

Was she lying on the floor with Holly? There was no way Maggie could get out. She quickly dialled her sister's number as she had minutes previously to tell her exactly what to do when Holly arrived. Sascha's voice had trembled as she'd agreed. She'd thought Maggie's initial text had been a joke.

Voicemail.

Maggie banged hard on the steel above her. 'Help!' But she knew even the occupants of the nearest house wouldn't hear. She had to call the police. If Penny was out in the freezing cold she couldn't hesitate. She dialled 911.

'Which service?'

Penny started screeching.

'Police, this is urgent!' There would be nobody around to find them.

'Just transferring you.'

'Don't,' Holly weakly murmured.

'Holly?' Maggie put her ear closer to the lid. 'Holly?'

The car bounced as weight moved off it.

'Hang up the phone.'

Maggie immediately complied. 'Done. I thought you'd… for god's sake make sure Penny's OK!' She heard Holly comforting her and eventually her weeping subsided.

'That was a stupid thing to do, Maggie.'

Maggie blinked as something thumped on the car. *Holly's fist?*
'What's happened to Sascha?'

'I think…' Holly still seemed drowsy. 'I think I might have
killed her.'

CHAPTER THIRTY-THREE

Maggie's chest tightened, her circulation suspended. She'd told Sascha to find something heavy and ambush Holly when she arrived. It was her fault. 'What did you do?' she spat. Now she felt even more powerless. She had to get free.

'I took her weapon. And used it.' Holly's voice was smudgy.

Maggie tried to straighten inside the trunk. 'Let me out. I have to help her.'

'It's too late. We have to keep going. Penny has to come with us now.'

'I'll do anything you want. Just open the trunk.' If Holly was delirious she could overpower her and wrestle Penny away. 'Quick, I can't breathe in here.'

'I'm going to release the catch and lift the door two inches. Throw your phone out.'

Maggie considered whether she should boot the lid out as soon as it was unlocked, but didn't want to risk it if Penny was in the way.

The trunk clicked and rose slightly so the weak yellow streetlight filled the crack.

'Toss it out.'

Maggie put her hand through with the phone, dropped it and withdrew her fingers. It clattered onto the street. When Holly bent to retrieve it she might be able to clip her with the door, but she was still fearful of striking Penny.

The door thudded back into place. Holly had rammed it down.

'What are you doing?' She heard Holly stamping on her cell.

'You're going to stay in there now.'

'Let me out!'

'You both have to come with me.'

'We can't take Penny with us!'

'We wouldn't have… but that was your choice.' Holly still sounded dazed.

'You can't drive and keep an eye on her!'

'I'll strap her in. She'll be fine,' Holly said bluntly. The rear passenger door opened, and Holly whispered to Penny as she secured her.

'Please, let me sit with her!'

'No more favours,' Holly growled.

'Call an ambulance for Sascha!'

'No.'

The door slammed.

The Scion bounced as Holly got in the driver's side, shut the door and started the engine. Maggie rolled to the back of the trunk as it accelerated and then sideways as the car turned and shot back the way they'd come. She anchored herself and turned so she was facing the back seat. She'd already tried kicking her way through it, but now all she wanted to do was check on Penny. 'Penny!' she called over the gunning engine. 'Penny, it's OK! I'm right here!'

Her constrained weight pitched again as they turned another corner. They weren't far from the address Babysitter had given them. *Had Holly really killed Sascha?* If her sister had attacked maybe she had no choice. She couldn't hear Penny. Maggie yelped as the vehicle shuddered hard down a ramp. She could make out the satnav voice instructing Holly.

'Next left. Then next right.'

The movement of her body corresponded and soon the Scion was slowing. Holly wouldn't be stupid enough to drive right up to the door. That's if wherever it was had a door.

The engine was switched off, and the suspension lifted as Holly got back out.

No traffic. Wait, she could discern the lap of water. They must be down at the wharf. 'Speak to me, Holly.'

She didn't reply but footfalls moved away from the car.

'Do you want me to scream and give us all away!'

Boots marched back. 'Shut up.'

She was right outside the trunk now. 'Let me out of here.'

'Wait.' The door clicked and sprang open.

Maggie was looking down the barrel of the Browning. Holly's expression was set hard above it. Seconds passed and Maggie waited for the bullet.

'Get out.'

Something had changed in Holly's demeanour. Maybe it was because there was no longer any part of her that trusted Maggie or because her daughter might be close by. Her eyes didn't blink as Maggie extricated herself and stood upright.

The car was parked on the edge of a waterside lot. The trawler jetty was on the opposite side of the port. Flakes melted into the inky black water between and in the distance lights coruscated where a handful of men moved around the moored boats. Maggie and Holly were standing about five hundred yards away from them in the deep shadow of a clock tower.

'Move or say anything now and Penny is an orphan.' Holly kept the gun pointed shakily at the middle of Maggie's chest.

Maggie could see she was overwrought. She opened her mouth to protest, but had second thoughts. She'd been in this position once. Perhaps this time she wouldn't be so lucky.

'Behind me, Loft 7, that's where you're going. Walk along the wharf and go inside. Take this phone with you. Passcode is 050516.' She handed Maggie her iPhone. 'I'm going to take Penny and find someplace else to watch. 'If he's tracking the phone he probably knows exactly where we've parked up.'

Maggie shook her head. 'I'm not leaving her.'

Holly raised the barrel so it was pointing at her face. She took in a wavering breath. 'Don't come out of there without Abigail.'

'Why would he bring her here? This has to be a trap.'

'There's only one way off the jetty. If he leaves, I'll follow.'

'And take Penny with you?'

'If I have to. Go. And tell him our silence is guaranteed if he frees her.'

'You know this won't work.' Maggie regarded the weapon and wondered which was her best option – obeying Holly or trying to get the gun out of her hand. If she'd killed Sascha, Maggie wouldn't hesitate to use it. But with Penny close by could she risk any shots being fired?

'Go,' Holly repeated.

Maggie strode slowly past the car and looked in through the window at Penny. Their eyes locked, and Penny beamed obliviously. Maggie tried to smile back and felt a pang in her throat. *Would it be the last time she'd see her?*

'I'm watching you every step of the way.'

She paced stiffly past the car, and the front seat obscured Penny's face. Then she set off along the lit edge of the wharf to the row of battered wooden fishing lofts. Maggie's sight blurred but she wouldn't allow the tears to come. She was coming back to get her daughter, by whatever means necessary.

CHAPTER THIRTY-FOUR

Holly watched Maggie advance through the heavy snowfall and follow the perimeter of the illuminated wharf before pocketing her Browning and taking Penny out of her seat. She grumbled but didn't cry, and Holly clutched her carefully and headed out of the lot. She limped along the road beside it and wondered if Sascha had properly come round.

After she'd wrestled the saucepan off her and knocked her unconscious, she'd checked the house and confirmed she was there on her own. Holly had dragged her inside the front door and quickly tied her up with an extension cord she'd found in the drawer in the hallway. She was moaning and groggy when she left.

But she couldn't tell Maggie the truth. If she believed Holly was capable of killing Sascha it made her more obedient. She touched the back of her head and examined her fingers. No blood but the area pulsed slowly under the skin as if it were too tight for the bruise expanding there. Her hand and arm still buzzed from the saucepan blows.

Holly staggered up an incline bordered by the lower garages of houses on the right-hand side and halted where there was a concrete platform with a park bench. She was elevated about twenty feet above the lot and could see across to the jetty.

She checked her watch.

2:01 a.m.

Less than five hours until sunrise.

Maggie hit the other side of the port and continued swiftly past the shuttered seafood stalls on the jetty until she reached the row of two-storey lofts.

Holly observed her looking up at the large numbers and stopping outside seven. Then she hesitantly pushed the door and slipped inside the dark recess that Holly briefly saw before it closed behind her.

Holly counted the seconds in her head. *Give her time. Was Babysitter really waiting?* She doubted he'd put himself at risk like that. *So what was the purpose of sending them here?*

A minute passed and she still hadn't emerged. *What if Maggie didn't come out? Was he expecting Holly to go over to investigate?* She scanned the garage doors behind her and then the dark windows in the houses above. She returned her attention to the jetty. If he harmed Maggie she didn't have another move. He still had Abigail.

Something was going on though. If the loft were empty Maggie surely would have been back through the door by now.

A forklift truck laden with white plastic boxes of fish headed away from the boats and moved slowly along the jetty.

Penny's breath was warm against the side of Holly's neck. She gently rubbed her back.

The entrance was still firmly closed. Holly knew she had to stand her ground and not be tempted to go over there.

But after another minute had passed she wondered if it had been a good idea to stamp on Maggie's iPhone. They could have opened FaceTime to enable her to hear what was going on.

Maggie had her phone – but after her trick with Sascha could she be trusted with it? If she didn't make it out Holly had no line of communication with Babysitter. *Shit, she'd been too eager to have Maggie get the phone away from her so she wouldn't be tracked.*

Still no sign of Maggie. A group of the fishermen sauntered along the jetty in their waterproofs and yellow boots leaving only one visible fisherman on the deck of the smallest trawler.

How long should she wait? Until the door opened, she decided. If he was in there and had attacked Maggie, he had to come out again.

CHAPTER THIRTY-FIVE

Maggie had already checked out half the loft. She hadn't been able to locate a light switch so had turned on the flashlight of Holly's phone. The expansive wooden structure was used for storage, and there were large nets suspended by ropes from the beamed ceiling. They hung down like blue and red curtains, and the smell of stale fish and sea salt was potent as she nervously weaved her way through them.

'Are you in here?' she asked for the third time. Her shoulder nudged one of the heavy nets, and it swung in a circle.

The beams creaked overhead as it swayed and cast animated shadows above.

'Answer me or I'm leaving.'

None came.

Maggie held her breath. This had to be an ambush, and she was unarmed. There had been no point asking for her snubbie to be returned. Holly knew she would put a bullet in her for what she did to Sascha. She had to bite down hard on those emotions. Holly would answer for it eventually, but she had to focus on escaping this place alive and getting back to Penny. She continued working her way through the nets, anticipating somebody pouncing any moment.

The phone buzzed in her hand, and she nearly dropped it. It was a text.

Why do you have Holly's phone?

Maggie arced the flashlight around. He'd seen her with it, which meant he was near. *But how near?* Her fingers trembled as she replied:

I'm here to negotiate.

When she sent it, she dreaded hearing it arrive. There wasn't a sound, however.

He answered seconds later.

If Holly's decided not to participate she can't care about her daughter.

Maggie had to think only of Abigail and realised how careful she had to be with her next response.

Holly worried what would happen to Abigail if we both walked into a trap.

There was a long pause before his retort came.

Perhaps you already have.

Maggie darted the flashlight around her, waiting for the attack to come out of the dark. Her phone vibrated.

There's something waiting for you at the back of the loft.

All her instincts told her to turn on her heel.

If the safety of both children is important…

Babysitter wasn't going to let her go. Even if she ran out now, he would still come after her and Penny. She wondered if Holly had spotted Babysitter in whichever place he was positioned to watch the loft. But, even if she had, Maggie had to find what he'd left there for them.

She snaked through the remaining nets until she reached the rear wall and played her flashlight over what she discovered there. On a low, paint-spattered table was a cardboard shoebox. Maggie didn't want to open it and remained where she was. She dreaded to think what was inside.

The phone pulsed.

All yours.

Maggie still didn't take another pace. And now she was sure Babysitter wasn't in the loft. *Why would he be? They could have called the cops.*

Why not take a peek? If Holly is being a fraidy cat doesn't mean you have to be…

Maggie swallowed drily and apprehensively approached the box.

CHAPTER THIRTY-SIX

Holly felt a wave of relief when the door opened and Maggie emerged. She'd been in there eight minutes. Something must have happened inside, but she was too far away to gauge her expression. She strode purposefully back along the wharf, but Holly kept her attention on the loft.

She would wait to see what Maggie had to say but nobody was getting off the jetty without her knowing. Keeping her focus on the entrance she made her way down the incline to the parking lot and waited for Maggie to join her in the shadow of the clock tower.

She stroked Penny's back as Maggie arrived but didn't shift her sight from Loft 7. 'What happened?'

'Nothing.'

'Nothing's taken you eight minutes?'

'I searched the place. He's not in there.'

Holly slid her gaze briefly to Maggie's. 'What deal did you make?'

'I just told you, he wasn't there. Let me have Penny.' She advanced a couple of steps.

'Stay where you are.' Holly held the Browning on her. 'Tell me the truth.'

'I have. He's probably watching us.'

Holly shot her eyes back to the loft. When she returned them to Maggie she'd pulled a black Ruger handgun from her puffer jacket.

'You know for sure I won't hesitate, Holly.' Her arm extended straight and taut.

'You can't shoot me. Not when I'm holding Penny.'

Maggie directed the handgun at her knees.

'What if I drop her?'

'I'll take that chance. Or you can just hand her over. She's all I want. Just do it.'

A cold snowflake stuck to Holly's bottom lip. 'I didn't kill Sascha.'

'Bullshit.'

Holly regretted the lie. Now Maggie had another reason to open fire. 'I promise you; I told you that because I needed you to think I could. I tied her up.'

'Why the hell should I believe you?'

'We can send the cops to the house.'

'You'll say anything to save yourself.'

'Anything to save Abigail. I couldn't kill *you* and her life depended on it. I give you my word about Sascha. If we don't step away from this, he's won. Can't you see that's why he handed you a weapon?'

'He wasn't in there. He'd just left this.'

'And now we're going to gift wrap his way out of this by killing each other.'

'If you don't let go of Penny now you'll leave me no choice.'

'Here.' Holly knew she had to make a move before Maggie did. She lowered her gun hand. 'Take her.' She twisted her body so she could lift her away.

Maggie warily walked forward and grabbed Penny. Clutching her daughter tight she swiftly reversed and, frowning, kept her Ruger on Holly.

Holly had come to a momentous decision. 'If either of us pulls the trigger d'you think the survivor is going to be allowed to escape? We've got to regain control.'

'We've never had any.'

'You're right.' Holly kept her pupils coupled to Maggie's. 'And he's just waiting for us to kill each other so he can do this to the next women he's targeted.'

'He has Abigail. You can't negotiate with him.'

'Give me the phone.' Holly stuck out her palm. 'Come on; I gave you Penny. If he's watching us then at least let's give him the impression that we trust one another. He wants us at each other's throats. Hand it over.'

Maggie readjusted Penny, but didn't give her the phone.

Holly dumped her Browning on the snow.

Maggie was impassive. 'You still have mine.'

Holly took the snubbie from her left pocket and dropped that too. 'Perhaps he could pick us both off now, but I don't think he came prepared for that. He thought *we*'d take care of it. Give me the phone.'

Maggie regarded the two weapons on the ground and chewed her lip. Swapping the Ruger to her left hand, but keeping it on Holly, she slipped out the phone and threw it over.

Holly caught it and typed a message.

No more guns. And neither of us is cooperating until I know Abigail is safe.

Holly read it aloud then sent it.

'You're only playing for time.'

'I'm not playing.'

Maggie breathed her daughter's scent, her nose in her hair.

Babysitter shot back an answer.

Holly, if you pick up your gun and kill Maggie now Abigail will be back in your arms in less than half an hour.

The coarse flakes fell silently at their feet.

CHAPTER THIRTY-SEVEN

'Says I can have Abigail back if I kill you.' But Holly didn't intend to make a move towards the guns.

'So what are you gonna do?' Maggie looked down at the weapons. Hers was back in her right hand.

'That depends on you. You could walk out of here with Penny now, but you know that'll only be a temporary reprieve.'

Maggie glanced around them, as if she might spot Babysitter, but kept her grip on the Ruger.

'Gonna pull the trigger for him? Drop it now, and we can find another way.'

Maggie shook her head, as if Holly were foolish. 'And what if I do? What then?'

'He has to talk to us.'

'I just want out of this.'

'If you shoot me in cold blood, d'you really think that'll be the end? Stop behaving the way he wants you to. You've got Penny. This is a bigger decision for me. Lose the gun. I'm telling the truth about Sascha.'

Maggie briefly closed her eyes then lowered her arm.

'OK.' Holly took an uneven breath and typed a message.

Anything happens to either of us and the other goes to the police. Give me back Abigail now and our silence is guaranteed.

She read it aloud to Maggie and sent it.

The phone vibrated.

Go to the police with what?

Holly read out Babysitter's reply then hers before sending.

With confirmation the East County Slayer is several women.

He responded seconds later.

Behind every successful man stands a woman.

Holly read it out.

'So what now?' Maggie asked after a minute had passed.

Holly prayed their tiny sliver of leverage would give him cause to reconsider. *Did he really want the truth about the Slayer to be exposed?*

Her phone buzzed again.

Tell Maggie if she doesn't shoot you I'll be coming for Penny.

'What does he say?'

Should she lie? But Holly understood it was crucial they both stop trying to trick each other. 'He's threatening Penny if you don't kill me.'

Maggie inhaled slowly.

Holly knew they'd reached the turning point. Surely Maggie had to see that she and Penny would forever be in danger even if she did follow his instructions. 'Make the decision, Maggie.'

Maggie exhaled, clenched her jaw and then made a show of deliberately tossing the gun so it came to rest with the others.

Holly felt her muscles slightly relax but neither of them spoke as they awaited Babysitter's response.

Congratulations. Abigail dies.

'Well?'

But Holly could barely maintain her balance as the lot seemed to shift beneath her. Three weapons lay only feet away from her. Maggie was defenceless. She could scramble for one of the guns, and Babysitter would witness her gesture of obedience and spare Abigail. She suspected Maggie had done exactly what she'd had to do in order to save Penny's life.

But Holly reminded herself that even though Maggie had obeyed when Penny had been taken he'd still attempted to have her murdered.

She had to remain defiant. Keep the channel open and try to find another way of getting Abigail back. But Maggie had to have guessed his last message and what Holly was contemplating.

Maggie's attention shifted to the guns.

She was nearer than Holly but had Penny to carry. But if she got to a weapon before Holly and fired, Abigail would be at the mercy of Babysitter. Holly fought back the compulsion and remained motionless.

One step forward and Maggie would quickly follow but the temptation to act built inside Holly until it felt like her chest would explode.

CHAPTER THIRTY-EIGHT

The phone hummed in Holly's hand.

Last chance. Kill Maggie. You've got ten seconds.

'He's given me ten seconds to do it.' Holly internally counted down.

Maggie shifted her foot.

'Please… don't.'

A severe gust blew in off the sea.

Holly hit zero, and her breath halted in her chest.

Another message arrived.

Your choice. Await further instructions.

'Well.' Maggie was still keyed up.

Holly told her. 'Get rid of the gun he gave you. I wouldn't trust it. And pick up yours.'

Maggie looked around, as if it might be a trick.

'We can't leave them lying here.'

Maggie stepped forward with Penny, and Holly went rigid as she reached the firearms.

Maggie booted the Ruger, and it slid across the lot, over the edge of the wharf and into the dark water. Then she bent down and picked up her snubbie.

Holly didn't blink.

She ejected the bullets from the cylinder onto the ground and pocketed it. Then she repeated the procedure with Holly's magazine. 'You collect them.' She took three paces back.

Holly walked six, bent to her knees and scraped all the bullets up. She stood and put Maggie's in the left pocket of her poncho and hers in the right. *Was Maggie really onside?* It was a demonstration of trust. Now neither could fire a shot without the other.

Babysitter sent another message.

Get back in your car and drive out of here. I'll tell you where you're going.

Holly answered:

I want proof Abigail is safe.

Ask me that again and she dies.

Holly showed Maggie what had been said.

She squinted at it. 'We'd better move.' Maggie cocked her head to the Scion. 'You've pushed things enough already.'

Holly eventually nodded. *Where was Abigail locked up?* She unsuccessfully tried to banish the image of her daughter alone in the dark calling out to her.

'We'll do as he says.' Maggie cupped the back of her daughter's head. 'Come on, I want to get Penny back in the car.'

Holly followed her to the Scion.

'I'll drive.' Maggie was already heading for the back seat to strap Penny in.

Holly wondered if she could really believe her. But after her gesture with the guns and bullets she hoped Maggie had figured they both had to take control of the situation or be forever anticipating Babysitter finding new candidates to eliminate them.

Holly slid into the passenger seat. *Was Babysitter still watching them and had he any intention of returning Abigail?* Maggie had Penny but she still doubted the story of her return. Holly had defied him and knew it wouldn't go unpunished. *But did he really know where they were headed or was he hastily improvising?*

She touched the wound at the back of her head and flinched before dialling 911. 'Police.'

Maggie dropped into the driver's seat. 'What are you doing?'

'I want to report a break-in at 335 Prospect Drive, Brentwood, Astley.' Holly sat upright as the operator questioned her. 'I'm a neighbour. Just… please hurry.' She hung up. 'She might have even gotten free by now. Knocked her out cold with the same saucepan she tried to brain me with, on your instructions.'

'You would have done the same.'

'Maybe.' But she could tell Maggie was still to be convinced. 'When I left her she was already coming round. Give the police time to head over there and then call her. She's gonna have a bruise the same size as mine but, I promise you, she's OK.'

CHAPTER THIRTY-NINE

'The murders of the East County Slayer are orchestrated by a man who calls himself Babysitter. He kidnaps children and demands their mothers commit murder to get them back. He then abducts another and forces their mother to kill the last woman he targeted, silencing one killer and creating another who stays silent for the sake of their child. I am one of those mothers, and my daughter Abigail has been taken. If I don't murder Maggie Walsh, Abigail's life has been threatened. Maggie and I have elected not to follow his instructions and are attempting to get Abigail back, and this video recording is a safeguard…'

Maggie looked across from the wheel and found Holly was biting her lip to hold back her emotions. She knew what sort of turmoil she was going through, but after her stand against Babysitter realised Holly had more resilience than she'd given her credit for. 'Finish it.'

Holly gulped and relayed the specifics of the night to her iPhone before stopping the recording.

Maggie noticed she wasn't wearing the surgical gloves any more. *Did that signify she was no longer intending to murder her?*

'I'll open my Hotmail account and send it via there.'

'Who's it going to?'

'Myself. And you. We can't include the cops yet. What's your email address?'

Maggie told her. 'So, if we don't make it home have you got someone who's likely to find it in your inbox?'

'No. But I'm also shooting it off to a lawyer I know.'

'Do it.' Maggie shifted gear as the Scion struggled back up the hill they'd entered Astley by and turned on the wipers to clear the snow obscuring the windshield. She glimpsed in the rear-view mirror for anyone following. There wasn't, and Penny was fast asleep. Maggie eyed the guns she'd put on the dash but didn't feel reassured by them. 'So how come you know a lawyer?'

Holly kept tapping the screen and didn't answer for a few seconds. 'It's my day job.'

Maggie realised she had no idea who she was sharing a car with. *Was Holly really a single mother Babysitter had randomly chosen? Or did they both have some connection to him?*

The car levelled off.

'I promise I'll do everything in my power to keep Penny safe if you promise to do the same for Abigail.' Holly finished typing.

Maggie nodded. 'Deal.'

Holly jabbed the screen. 'Gone. To Greg Weintraub at Link, Hooper and Pearce.'

'You can rely on him?'

'He won't get it until Monday. I've told him to call me at home then. If he can't reach me, he's to open it. Now level with me.'

'About what?'

'Janet Braun.'

Maggie rolled them to a standstill at a fork in the road. 'Which way?'

'Did you kill her?'

Should she really tell her the truth? 'No.'

'Babysitter gave Penny back to you – just like that?'

'Why wouldn't he? He was sending you into my house right after.'

'That's the truth?'

'That's the truth.' It wasn't, but Maggie knew that now was exactly the wrong time to share it. 'I've told you what happened.' But the fact was she'd lied to Holly about that night, and wondered if she would have to become the person she'd been in Janet Braun's home once again. She was still trying to build walls around that moment, but could still see herself slinking into the bedroom. Only keeping Penny safe and considering the time it had bought Maggie to spend with her could momentarily block out what she'd made herself do.

Holly sucked her lips, as if giving Maggie the opportunity to rethink her reply.

Maggie didn't.

'If we're to work out who's doing this we can't afford to conceal anything from each other.'

'I understand that but I don't know how many different ways I can answer the same question.'

Holly sighed.

'Which way?' Maggie revved the engine to keep it turning over as snow scudded across the white road ahead. 'We can't sit here all night.'

Holly checked the phone. 'Nothing.'

'Maybe I should pull off.'

'I'll send him a message.'

CHAPTER FORTY

Where are we going?

Holly read it out, hit send and pointed to the shuttered 'Garganta Burger' stand just beyond the right fork. 'We could park up there while we wait.' She suspected Maggie was still lying about Janet but, at least for the moment, they weren't trying to kill each other.

She glanced at the dash.

2:31 a.m.

Less than four and a half hours until sunrise.

'Company.'

Holly followed Maggie's gaze to the mirror. There was a vehicle approaching them from behind. As it drew close, Maggie squinted against the glare of the headlights.

'They're out late.' Maggie didn't move her eyes from it.

'Could be a fisherman.' But Holly swivelled and studied the shadow in the driving seat. It was a midnight blue Nissan Frontier pickup, and it braked only half a foot from them.

Maggie was about to take off when it honked harshly at them. It swerved around and surged by.

Holly strained to catch the driver's face but the Nissan quickly accelerated past the burger stand.

The road was quiet again, the snow falling even harder.

'So, do we hang fire over there?' Maggie turned the wheel.

A message arrived from Babysitter.

Follow.

Holly's attention whipped back to the receding lights just as they rounded a bend. 'That was him. He wants us to go after him.'

Maggie stayed put. 'He's drawing us into a trap.' She regarded her daughter in the mirror. 'I'm not taking Penny to him.'

Holly knew she'd feel the same way. 'OK, let's stay behind him and see where he takes us. The minute we're not sure, we stop the car.'

'We need to get Penny somewhere safe.'

'OK. Let's consider where but we can't lose him now.'

Maggie was torn. 'She should be with Sascha.'

'She *should* be,' Holly said significantly. 'But that's past. We have to move now or we'll lose him.'

Maggie still didn't budge. 'The minute I suspect we're in danger, we're pulling over.'

'Agreed.' Holly contemplated the darkened road ahead.

Maggie shot after the pickup.

A few moments later they spotted the twin red glow from the Nissan. The trees opened up and suddenly they were on a wide expanse with white fields either side. But visibility got poorer as they drove against a squall.

'He's leading us out into the middle of nowhere.' Maggie shook her head, as if she was about to give in to her reservations.

'I'll contact him.'

Where are you taking us?

She didn't expect a response, but one came immediately.

Hexham.

Holly informed Maggie and consulted the satnav. 'That's about four miles from here.'

'I know it. Not much there but salt marshes.' Maggie had caught up with the pickup, but decelerated to open up the distance between them again.

They were now about a hundred yards from the Nissan; Holly appreciated Maggie wouldn't want to get any closer. 'It's a straight road into Hexham. He won't be able to spring any surprises before we get there.'

'Let's not assume anything.' Maggie hunched forward so she could focus on the vehicle.

'He's improvising, expected things to be over at the wharf.'

'We shouldn't underestimate him. He's probably got a backup plan.' She flicked the wiper speed up to max.

Holly shared her trepidation. *Did he know exactly what he was doing, or was he luring them somewhere remote and devising plan B in the meantime?* He still had Abigail, so he was assured that at least Holly would follow. 'Maybe…' she was thinking out loud, 'I should go in alone this time.'

Maggie said nothing but checked Penny in the back seat.

'He wants to silence us both. If it's just me that goes into Hexham, I can tell him you'll go to the cops if anything happens.'

Maggie chewed it over, and Holly could tell she was sorely tempted, for Penny's sake.

'But like he says, with what? We still have no idea who he is or why he's doing this.'

Holly wondered if Maggie was still afraid to go to the police because of implicating herself in whatever had happened to Janet Braun. 'We have his licence plate.' She nodded towards it, but the numbers weren't visible through the darkness and snow. 'If we get a little closer.'

'That's probably exactly what he wants. And something tells me that's not going to make any difference.'

'You need to get Penny somewhere safe.'

'I can't drop you in the middle of nowhere.'

Holly acknowledged how swiftly the dynamic had changed. *Or was that more to do with Maggie not wanting the death of another mother on her conscience?* 'You could drop me on the outskirts once he's told us where he wants us to go.'

But at that moment Babysitter's pickup squealed to a halt.

Maggie stamped on the brake, but they skidded nearer to the Nissan.

Babysitter's vehicle skewed on the wet snow before righting itself. Their Scion froze about thirty feet away.

'Load the guns.' Maggie put the car into reverse and jerked them back.

Holly's fingers were already retrieving the bullets from both pockets.

'Shit!' Maggie had lost control, and they skated sideways.

The front tipped up, and the Scion juddered to a standstill.

'We're in a ditch.' She gunned the engine, but the wheels couldn't get any traction. Maggie passed Holly's Browning to her and opened the cylinder of her snubbie. 'Hurry.'

Holly passed Maggie her bullets, and she snatched them out of her palm. She fumbled her own into the magazine. Holly peered through the snow. Their headlights no longer illuminated the pickup. *Had he got out?* She slid the magazine hard into place.

The doors clunked as Maggie locked them.

Snow churned outside while the engine ticked over.

CHAPTER FORTY-ONE

Maggie fumbled the last bullet into the chamber of the snubbie, her eyes bouncing between it and the windshield. No figure emerging from the snow. 'He might be circling around us.' Her attention darted to the side window and then to Penny in the back seat. She'd half woken. 'Ssshhh.'

Holly took her safety off. 'Try again.'

Maggie accelerated hard, but still couldn't free the Scion.

'Should I get out and push?'

'No. Stay inside.' Maggie pumped the pedal.

'Perhaps he doesn't know we've come off the road.'

'He does now.' She stopped gunning the engine.

'If we do nothing he'll definitely find us.'

'Don't open the door.' Maggie hefted her weapon and aimed it at the windshield.

'So what do we do, just stay here and wait for him?'

The phone vibrated.

Holly read the message aloud: '"Do you need assistance?"'

'Son of a bitch.' Maggie's gaze shifted to the rear window then Penny. 'It's okay, sweetheart.'

'Doesn't mean he's still in his car either.'

Maggie switched off the engine and wipers. 'Just listen.'

They both strained their ears for feet crunching snow, but the wind surged against the Scion.

Holly held up her hand. 'Is that the pickup?'

Maggie could just discern the low rumble of the Nissan. She told herself she should have heeded her instincts and stayed at the fork. Or taken Holly up on the offer of letting her go to Hexham alone. Now she'd endangered her daughter again. Her finger rested against the trigger. It was stiff and she knew she had to pull on it long and hard. *Would he try to pick them both off?*

Another message alert.

Maggie fixed the whiteout before them. 'What does he say?'

'"Go to the middle of Hexham town square. I won't be there, but a part of my life will."'

A car door slammed.

'Hear that?' Holly swallowed tightly.

They both held their breaths.

An engine revved.

'That's him. Let me push us out.' Holly started to unlock her door.

Maggie grabbed her shoulder. 'No. Wait.'

Holly stiffened.

Maggie loosened her grip, but Holly remained rigid.

Tyres hissed on the snowy road and then Babysitter's headlights swung in their direction.

'He's coming at us!' Maggie trained the gun on the vehicle.

But the beams angled away as the pickup straightened and barrelled back the way it had come.

The drone of the engine receded.

They remained silent as a whistle of breeze swallowed the last traces of the Nissan.

'He's gone back towards Astley. It's got to be a trick,' Holly said eventually.

Maggie nodded. 'If there's more than one of them someone could still be here.'

'I only saw one person in the pickup though.'

'You're sure of that?'

'Pretty sure.' But Holly didn't sound it.

A minute ticked by.

'We can't stay here all night.' Holly pocketed her Browning, unlocked the door and let the storm in.

'Come back!'

But Holly had slid out, and Maggie heard her stagger to the rear of the car.

'Start it up again!' she shouted over the gale.

Maggie complied and increased the pressure on the pedal.

'I can see where it's—'

Maggie lost the remainder of the sentence. 'What?' she yelled at the open door.

The Scion suddenly lurched forward, and Maggie took her foot off the pedal. But it was still rolling across the road. There could be a ditch the opposite side. Maggie hit the brakes, jerked the wheel, and the car skidded and turned forty-five degrees before coming to a halt. She was now pointed towards Hexham. Maggie squinted through the open door, but couldn't see further than a few feet. 'Holly!'

A shape emerged from the maelstrom. It was Holly, and she quickly jumped back into the car and pulled the door closed.

'Lock it.' Maggie checked on Penny again. She was blinking with confusion. Maggie felt the cold envelop her and shivered inwardly. 'Let's take off.' She moved them carefully forward, peering through the arcing wipers for signs of anyone nearby.

'Step on it. At least until we're clear.'

Maggie guided them to the middle of the road.

Holly glanced over her shoulder.

'Keep an eye out. He could easily come back and surprise us.'

The windshield was suddenly bathed in bright light, and Maggie yanked the wheel as two headlights headed straight for them.

The truck honked a late warning.

Maggie wrenched the car to the side of the road as the rig rumbled past, its cargo of felled trunks swerving behind it as it passed.

'Jesus.' Holly was frozen as they came to a standstill.

Maggie swiftly turned the wheel again, accelerated and moved them off the edge of the road before the car could glide into the ditch once more. Her heart was leaping hurdles, and she waited for it to slow. 'This is madness. We can't even see a foot in front of us.'

Holly consulted the satnav. 'Hexham's only three or so miles from here.'

Should they carry on? Babysitter had gone back the opposite way. 'We could all get killed before we get there.'

'Let's see if we can get Penny somewhere safe.' Holly pulled on her belt.

'In Hexham? There's nothing there but vacation homes.'

'Maybe you can contact your friend, Sascha.'

Maggie was relieved that Holly had again confirmed Sascha was alive. 'She's my sister.'

Holly shook her head. 'I'm sorry. I could call her and get her to come meet us.'

Maggie concentrated on the road. 'OK. Call her at home now.' She gave Holly the number.

Holly quickly dialled. 'Better you talk to her. I'll put it on speaker.'

But the phone went to voicemail.

Holly hung up. 'Perhaps she's with the police… or been taken to a hospital?'

But Maggie felt a stab of panic – what if Sascha hadn't been found alive? 'Try her cell.' She reeled off the number.

Holly dialled again.

'Hello?' Sascha answered breathless.

Maggie had never been so glad to hear her. 'Sascha, it's Maggie, you OK?'

'Where are you? That bitch attacked me and tied me up, but somebody called the police. Was that you?'

'No. That was the person who attacked you. I'm with her now.'

'The police told me your house is on fire and that you were taken by a woman at gunpoint.'

'Listen to me, Sascha. Are they still there?'

'Yes. I'm with a paramedic.' She lowered her voice. 'The officers are searching the yard.'

'Then hang up. Call me when you're alone.'

'Are you being held hostage?'

'No.'

'What about Penny?'

'She's with me. We're both safe.'

'Are you being forced to say this?'

'No. Really, I *am* fine. Just hang up now and call me when you can.'

There was a pause, and Maggie and Holly could hear the sound of a low male voice.

'Just say yes if you're in danger,' Sascha whispered.

'I'm not. Go somewhere private. I need you to pick up Penny as soon as you can.'

'OK. Sure you don't want me to tell the cops?'

'Please don't. Now hurry.'

Holly ended the call. 'She's got this number now. Feel better?'

Maggie felt her chest loosen. At least she'd established Sascha was safe.

'We'll wait for her to call us. Just get us to Hexham in one piece.'

Maggie rubbed away tiredness and the permanent image of the headlights on snow. 'What are you going to do once you get there?'

'Play his game,' Holly replied. 'Do whatever he needs me to do to get Abigail back.'

'You know she's not going to be there.'

'No. I don't,' Holly snapped.

'Well, we have to decide what we'll do if she's not.' Maggie couldn't leave Holly to face Babysitter alone; *but was she right about not handing them both on a plate?*

'Let's make it to the town square first.'

Maggie grasped the wheel tighter. 'There's only this one road in. Maybe he's just sending us somewhere until he's figured out how to dispose of us.'

The snow was building on the glass, the wipers unable to handle the flakes. Much harder and they'd be buried before they got there.

CHAPTER FORTY-TWO

One moment they had no light to guide them the next they could spot the sporadic yellow windows of occupied vacation homes fringing the marshes of Hexham. Once a thriving fishing town, the sea had been depleted until, by the 1960s, the only industry left was razor clams.

Deserted during the seventies and eighties, it had recently been given a new lease of life as a magnet for the wealthy seeking unblemished real estate for the construction of modern, upscale retreats.

Holly had an ex-boyfriend who had driven his dogs out here to walk them, but she hadn't been back since her teenage years. Main street now comprised of a general store and deli that supplied overpriced groceries to the closeted community and several restaurants that only they could afford to dine in. Reality very rarely impinged on the place, and that's how its residents liked it.

'I think I know how to get to the square.' Maggie eased the car down a ramp that led to the shoreline.

'When did *you* last visit?' Holly put her palm against the dash as they descended.

'Couple of years ago.' Maggie didn't elaborate.

'So, you know people here?'

'No. I came to… my father wanted his ashes scattered here.'

Holly didn't know how to respond.

'Depressing place. I never understood why he had such a fixation for it.'

'Maybe you're right. Perhaps Babysitter's tucking us away here until he's worked out what to do with us.'

Maggie rolled the car past Serendipity, a seafood restaurant with only the menus illuminated in the window. They entered a small plaza and through the snow could make out a lighthouse winking at the edge of the next cove.

'So what are we looking for here?' Maggie parked up against the kerb opposite the square.

The area was barely visible beyond the swirling flakes.

'I'll ask him.' Holly sent a message to Babysitter.

In Hexham. What next

After thirty seconds had passed, Holly grabbed the door handle. 'Wait—'

'Nobody has come in behind us. But in this weather, it's going to be hard to tell if they do. I'm going to quickly check it out.' Holly needed to move, couldn't be sitting still for a second while Abigail was in danger. 'Whatever Babysitter's motives are, I'm going to obey. Stay with Penny. I'll be as quick as I can.'

Maggie glanced to the back seat. Penny was sleeping. 'OK. I'll keep the engine running. How's that hip?' She nodded at the wound she'd inflicted.

Holly ignored the question and handed her the phone. 'In case Sascha calls. Or he gets in touch.'

Maggie took it. 'Five minutes. I don't know what he expects you to find. I'm sure this is just a distraction.'

As if in response, the phone buzzed. Maggie read the message and showed it to Holly.

Find me. Find Abigail.

'Watch out for other cars.' Holly opened the door and was assaulted by the freezing salt wind. She pulled up her hood, but it was immediately whipped off her head again. She jammed her

hands in her pockets, made sure there was no pickup coming down
the road behind them and then hobbled into the square, her body
leaning hard into a violent gust.

*Was Babysitter escaping with Abigail? What choice did she have
though?* Holly half closed her eyes as the blizzard lashed her face
and tried to see her booted feet through her cracked lids. It was a
couple of inches deep here, and when she peered up again Holly
could see drifts had already built up against the general store to
the west of the square.

As she hit the cobbled area she swivelled back to the Scion
and could only just perceive the twin lights. The engine noise was
drowned out and, over the air rumbling against her eardrums, she
heard a lone seagull as it was buffeted somewhere above. Holly
attempted to spot anything significant. The eddying snowfall only
allowed her to take in occasional glimpses of her surroundings,
however. The lighthouse flashed to her far right.

The bruise at the back of her head began to thud, and her injury
smarted again. It appeared the painkillers were wearing off. Her
teeth chattered against the cold.

As she progressed to the middle, a dark shape obscured her view
of the lighthouse. She headed for it and a statue materialised from
the blockade of white.

She blinked as she took in the dark dimensions of the three
spindly figures before her. They were faceless, their smooth features
impassive and eerie. Holly struggled to read what was carved into
the onyx plinth they were standing on.

In memoriam. To the 117 migrant workers who lost
their lives on Hexham salt marshes. Their toil and
sacrifice never forgotten.

*Was this what Babysitter intended her to find? And was he or the
drone monitoring her?* She circled the plinth and hunted for any
other inscriptions and came to a park bench the other side. On

a fine day it obviously presented a clear view across the flats. The seat was now covered in snow; a brass plate was screwed to the back of it. Holly wiped at the flakes partially concealing what was engraved there.

FOR TOM FRESNADE 1983–2012

Holly memorised the name and date. *Was any of this relevant?* She continued her circuit of the statue until she was facing the figures again, but there was nothing else written on the plinth.

Holly cut across the square and skirted the edge of it as her face stung and burnt. She followed the curb and covered the cobbles around the statue and bench. There was nothing else here, but this was where Babysitter had specified… *was he just toying with her?*

It was time to return to the car, and she squinted her eyes against the breeze as she searched for the headlights.

As she drew near Holly could hear the engine rev. Looking up she saw the Scion take off and accelerate at full speed towards her.

CHAPTER FORTY-THREE

Was Maggie still determined to kill her? The car was coming square at Holly, and it didn't matter which way she threw herself. But the Scion swerved to her right and headed for the exit on the other side of the square, cutting the corner as it did so.

'Wait!' Its rear lights vanished into the snow. Maybe Maggie had used the phone to speak to Sascha or just decided she didn't want to endanger Penny any longer. Blood pounded harder through the bruise on Holly's scalp. *What the hell would she do now?*

But the noise of another engine returned her attention to where the Scion had been parked. A set of lights burnt through the thick flakes, and she scurried back to the square. She swiftly made her way to the statue and hid behind the three figures.

Holly blinked against the wind as she watched the other vehicle slow. *Had Babysitter turned around and come into Hexham behind them?*

The headlights halted.

A metal door slid back.

Holly ducked as a figure climbed down.

The sound of a shutter opening quickly followed.

Holly cautiously crossed the square but as she drew nearer to the vehicle was relieved to find it was only a small white delivery truck with 'Gideon Fisheries' emblazoned along the side. A guy in yellow rubber dungarees was unloading some orange crates.

A car honked behind her. Holly swivelled and saw another set of headlights flash at her from the direction the Scion had disappeared. She scrambled for them and found Maggie waiting for her on the opposite corner.

'Sorry. I saw someone pull up behind me,' Maggie said as Holly dropped back into the passenger seat.

She yanked the door shut. 'It's just a guy delivering to the fish restaurant.'

'Did you find anything?'

'There's a statue to commemorate migrants who died on the marshes in the middle of the square.'

'People still drown here. The tide out there can come in real fast.' Maggie switched on the warm air.

Holly's face was too numb to feel it. 'I heard those stories. There was a bench with a name on it as well. Tom Fresnade.'

'Tom Fresnade?' Maggie frowned.

'Heard of him?'

Maggie shook her head.

'Looks like he might have lost his life on the marshes too. 1983 to 2012... 29 when he died.'

Maggie was already using the phone to Google him. '"Tom Fresnade. Hexham."' She enlarged the results with her fingers and read out what she'd found.

'"On 26th April 2012, Rich Temple and his two daughters were trapped on the Hexham salt marshes by the incoming tide. Tragically, one of the daughters, Milly, drowned, but due to the heroic actions of local, Tom Fresnade, Mr Temple and his eldest, Colette, were saved. However, when Tom Fresnade returned for Milly he also lost his life."'

'Anything more?' Holly leaned over to examine the phone.

Maggie scrolled. 'The story's on a few local sites. Here we are.' She skim-read. 'Tom Fresnade lived and worked in his family's business in Brinkley.'

'That's right near here.'

Maggie glanced up from the screen. 'Back the way we came.'

'Back the way Babysitter went.'

Maggie nodded. 'But let's just take a breath. Are we sure he'd expect us to find this information?'

'Here.' Holly took the phone from Maggie and typed a message to Babysitter.

Is Abigail in Brinkley

She showed it to Maggie and then sent it.

'So what do we do while we wait?'

'See if we can find anything else about Fresnade's family. There can't be many businesses with that name in Brinkley.' Holly put the name and the town in a search and perused the info. 'It's a smokery. 'Established 1968. ' She found a photo of a fragile old man in white overalls and paper hat surrounded by three young men in similar attire.

Maggie cast a look back into the square as the shutter was rolled back down on the truck.

'Maybe Babysitter has a connection to Tom Fresnade.' Holly had started to thaw.

'What about the father, Rich Temple?'

Holly put his name into a search but her phone rang.

Unknown caller.

She answered immediately. 'Hello?'

'It's Sascha.'

'Sascha, wait.' Holly hit speaker and put it on the dash. She didn't want this conversation to be private.

'Sascha, are you OK?' Maggie asked.

'I'll live. The police have just left, but I have to make a statement in the morning. What the fuck's going on?'

Holly wondered where Maggie would even start.

'It's a very complicated situation but I promise you Penny and I are safe.'

'I just spoke to the other woman, right?'

'Yes, I'm here,' Holly interjected. 'I'm sorry for what I had to do, but you didn't leave me any choice.'

'Who is she, Maggie?'

Maggie chewed her lip. 'Somebody who's in an even more desperate situation than I am. Look, we can trust her but I need you to come get Penny while I help her.'

Holly felt a surge of relief. Only minutes ago she thought Maggie had deserted her.

'Help her do what?'

'The less you know the better. Will you come?'

'I don't like this but of course I will. Where are you?'

Maggie narrowed her eyes at the phone. 'And you won't involve the police?'

There was a pause. 'If you say so.'

'I do. You have no idea what's at risk if you do. You've got to promise.'

'OK.'

'Promise, Sascha.'

Holly could almost feel the history between the two sisters as they spoke.

'I promise.'

'OK. We're in Hexham.'

'What the hell are you doing out there?'

'Can you drive here as soon as you can?'

The phone buzzed as a message arrived.

'Wait.' Maggie took the phone from the dash, read it and held it out to Holly.

In Brinkley. But not for long.

Maggie spoke at the mouthpiece. 'Scrap that. Meet us just outside Brinkley.'

'Brinkley? What's this about?'

'Bring some blankets for Penny. We're heading there now. What's the name of that steak place you like in Ebden?'

'The Grey Wolf.'

'We'll meet you in the lot. Careful on the roads, it's treacherous. But get there as soon as you can.'

'I'm leaving now.'

'You've promised no police, Sascha.'

'I know, I know. I'll call you if I'm held up.'

Maggie ended the call, handed the phone to Holly and put the car in drive.

'You don't have to come with me to Brinkley.' But Holly was sure she would, and the reassurance of that felt like the first positive element of her ordeal.

'I do. He's had time to arrange something while we've been here. .'

Maggie was right. He was still in control. Brinkley could be a trap, of course, but while there was still a dialogue with him and gas in the car she could maintain the hope they could negotiate Abigail back.

3:06 a.m.

Less than four hours until sunrise.

CHAPTER FORTY-FOUR

The return journey took them longer than Maggie anticipated. Visibility was almost non-existent and they both kept a watchful eye for Babysitter's car. He could easily ambush them coming back from Hexham, so when they found themselves behind a salt spreading truck Maggie stuck close to it until she spotted the first turn off that would take them to Brinkley.

Now they were alone, and there were no streetlights. The pines that lined the thin road were white laden, and the snow before them untouched.

'Hexham, now Brinkley.' Maggie clenched her fists around the wheel.

'Trying to find a connection?' Holly fought to find a comfortable sitting position.

'Maybe there isn't one. After all, Janet Braun was a stranger to me.'

'And you to me.' Holly wiped her nose. 'Perhaps he's just a misogynist getting off on manipulating women.'

'He's definitely an egotist. Maybe we should be pandering to it to get Abigail back.'

'How?'

Maggie put the fan on to clear the windshield. 'He clearly wants to show us who he is. He's been skulking in the background. Maybe operating in secret as the East County Slayer isn't reward enough. If he wants to let us in to how he thinks we have to take advantage of it.'

Holly's head darted back to the blackness beside her. 'I think I just saw a sign for Ebden – that's where the steak place is, right?'

'Blink and you'll miss it.' Maggie peered left. 'People only come this way if they want to find The Grey Wolf.'

'I've never heard of it.'

'It's just a steak and baked potato place but my sister likes to remind herself where she's from every once in a while.'

'She older than you?'

'Younger. We've nothing in common except we both love Penny. Here it is. Let's make sure the guns are out of sight.'

The sign was still lit, but the name and insignia were obscured by snow. The headlights swung around the car park at the side of the inn, which was in darkness.

'Doesn't look like she's made it yet.' Holly gritted her teeth and hissed.

'You OK?' Maggie saw pain register on her face.

'Think I need some more painkillers.'

'Sascha will have some. She's a walking drugstore.' It struck her that if she'd shot at the bedroom door a few more inches to the left she would have killed Holly. Things had changed so much in the last hour but she reminded herself what she'd been prepared to do for Penny. If it came down to it, she'd do the same again, and Maggie was sure Babysitter had already concocted a way of using their maternal instincts against them a second time.

'Look at her.' Holly regarded still-sleeping Penny. 'Don't you ever get jealous of how oblivious they are?'

Maggie could see how her daughter was a constant reminder of Abigail's absence. 'She'll be hungry soon.'

'So she hasn't spoken her first word yet?'

Maggie had forgotten she'd shared that. 'I've been told she will in her own time.'

'Are you still breastfeeding her?'

Maggie shook her head. 'I can't. I'm having chemo treatment.'

Holly turned to her, her expression stunned. 'But when you were locked in the bedroom…'

'I needed to plant that image to stop you attacking me.' There was movement at the entrance to the lot, and Maggie was relieved she didn't need to elaborate further. 'Here she comes.'

A silver Acura cleaved through the snow and parked beside them. The driver's door immediately opened, and Sascha emerged; her head was bandaged and she wore a pink quilted jacket.

Maggie got out of the car into the bitter air, and they embraced stiffly. 'Thanks for coming. You OK?' Her sister always smelt good.

Sascha quickly released her. 'Is Penny OK?' She squinted in through the back window of the car at the baby. 'She must be freezing.'

'She's fine.'

Without a word, Sascha went to her car and pulled a baby bag off the passenger seat.

This was how it always was. Like Sascha had taken over from her mother and was always silently despairing of every decision Maggie made.

'Let me wrap her properly before I take her out of the car.' Snow was already settling on Sascha's false eyelashes.

'She'll be fine.'

'We'll see.' Sascha circled around the car so she could get in beside Penny's seat.

Maggie took a breath and dropped back in the driver's seat. She closed the door the same time as her sister and, momentarily, nobody spoke as Sascha unzipped her bag, took out some blankets and draped them around Penny.

'There,' Sascha said, as if it were a job long overdue. 'So what have you got yourself mixed up in this time?'

'Where's Christian?' Maggie studied her in the mirror.

'In Atlanta.' It was Sascha's stock response.

Maggie was aware she and Christian were having major problems but knew better than to probe any further. 'You going to be OK coping on your own?'

'Natalia is coming tomorrow.'

That made Maggie feel better. Sascha's housekeeper had three daughters and was great with Penny. Even though she was a conscientious godmother, Sascha didn't have any natural instinct for childcare. After becoming bored with the lifestyle she'd willingly hemmed herself into she'd decided late that she wanted kids, and when she couldn't it had caused a rift between her and Christian.

'So how long before you pick her up?' It was usually a bone of contention between them. Sascha maintained that Maggie was overprotective and should let her spend more time with her niece, but tonight she didn't realise the implications of her question.

Maggie considered how to answer. 'As soon as I can.' She tried to keep the tremor out of her voice.

'Whatever it is that's going on between you two, I don't want to know. Just work it out.'

Maggie fleetingly wondered if Sascha would be happy if she never knocked on her front door again. They'd had the discussion about what would happen if her treatment failed. It was early days yet, but she knew she had to consider the worst-case scenario. Maggie didn't completely approve of Sascha's lifestyle – *did she really want Penny brought up in such a sterile, broken home?* But Sascha did love Penny, and none of the alternatives would guarantee Penny the security she knew her sister could offer. Maggie had proved to herself she would do anything to enjoy every second of motherhood she had but now it could already be time to say goodbye to her daughter.

'How's your head?' Sascha addressed Holly. 'Not as bad as mine I bet,' she added before the other woman could respond. 'I don't know who the hell you are but if Maggie doesn't come back in one piece I'll be calling the cops. I've seen your face.'

Maggie interrupted. 'I told you, Sascha—'

'We can talk about this later, Maggie. The priority is getting Penny back home safe.' Sascha unbelted Penny, and she immediately woke up and started to cry. 'No, no, no. It's all right. It's Auntie Sash.' She lifted her out of the chair and wrapped her in the blankets.

Maggie got out of the car, trudged around to the other side and opened the passenger door.

'Hold this.' Sascha proffered the bag.

Maggie ignored her and gently took Penny from her as she got out. She rested her face in the crook of her neck and lightly squeezed. 'It's OK, sweetheart.' She could feel her warm breath against her and allowed the tears to fill her eyes.

Sascha didn't notice and was hugging her collar tight to her throat as she waited. She stamped her feet.

'Be a good girl for Auntie Sash,' Maggie whispered. 'Love you.' She cuddled her and inhaled her skin.

'I'm freezing here,' Sascha said caustically.

Maggie told herself her sister didn't know what was going on. But she still felt anger spike. She held onto Penny for a little longer. There was no way this would be goodbye. She wouldn't allow that. She handed her back to Sascha.

'Come to Auntie Sash.'

'Take good care of her.'

But her sister was already moving to her car. She'd had a seat fitted for Penny in the back. It was more expensive than Maggie's. She opened the door, threw in the bag and belted Penny in before straightening. 'So where are you two going now?'

Maggie didn't respond.

Her sister narrowed her eyes. 'OK, I'm out of here.'

Before Sascha could seal the door, Maggie leaned in and kissed the top of Penny's warm head.

'OK?' Sascha said impatiently as Maggie stepped back again. She still hadn't noticed her sister was crying.

'Take care.' Maggie embraced Sascha, and she remained rigid.

When she released her Sascha was frowning. 'So when will we see you?' She blinked against the snowflakes.

Maybe she could see her tears. 'As soon as I can.' It was the truth.

'OK. Call me.' Sascha shut the back passenger door. 'But I'm free all weekend. I can keep Penny for as long as you need.'

'Thanks.'

'Then we'll talk,' she said sternly.

Maggie nodded then remembered. 'Do you have any painkillers on you?'

Sascha sighed and then pulled her handbag from between the seats. 'Tylenol?'

'Something stronger.'

Sascha scornfully shook her head and rummaged deeper, produced a yellow bottle and handed it over. 'They for her?'

Maggie nodded again and slid them into her pocket.

Sascha slammed her door, and the car started up and reversed back.

Maggie waved to her sister, but only got a withering look in return as Sascha spun the car and headed back to the entrance. Maggie watched her pull out and the headlights disappear before she got back into the Scion.

'You OK?'

Maggie sniffed. 'We'd better get going.'

'She obviously cares about you and Penny,' Holly mitigated. 'Sure you don't want to go with them?'

Maggie didn't answer.

'I wouldn't blame you if you did.'

'We finish this. Then I'm picking Penny up.' Maggie accelerated, dropped them back onto the road and took off in the opposite direction to her daughter.

CHAPTER FORTY-FIVE

Holly gagged as she dry swallowed one of the Demerol Maggie had given her. Her hip was burning again, and the back of her head was thumping so much it felt like she needed to pierce the skin to relieve the pressure.

'Always read the label,' Maggie hunched herself over the wheel so she could keep focussed on the road ahead.

'Do you trust your sister?'

'Penny will be fine with her.' Maggie seemed to be convincing herself.

Holly made sure the spiky flower head was still tucked up her right sleeve. She would need it again if the drugs didn't work. 'I mean not to call the police.'

'I was half expecting them to show up back there.'

Holly nodded. 'We can't afford for her to do that.'

'As long as she's got Penny to herself she's happy.'

'She doesn't have children?'

'Can't have them. We hardly spoke before I fell pregnant with Penny.'

'So where's Penny's father?' It was a question Holly had wanted to ask since she'd been watching her house.

'Jeff took off. Soon as I was diagnosed. Cancer and a baby, either of those on their own would be too much for some men.'

'Where is he now?'

'God knows. He's never met Penny.'

Holly shook her head. She hadn't had time to consider Maggie as a vulnerable human being. 'So what's the prognosis?'

'Not good. It's in one lung. Hard to believe such a tiny shadow can cause so much turmoil. Knew I shouldn't have tried that one cigarette at Rudy Tench's seventeenth birthday party.'

Holly felt ashamed that all she could think was that at least Maggie's daughter was safe. She would sacrifice any part of herself to be able to say the same of Abigail.

The car slid by a row of houses. Only a few windows were illuminated.

Maggie slowed the Scion. 'We're on the outskirts of Brinkley. Any suggestions?'

'I'll let him know we're here.' Holly sent a message to Babysitter.

In Brinkley. What next?

His reply was instant.

Lot 4. Splitrock Industrial Park.

Holly read it out and put it into the satnav. 'Three minutes away.'

Maggie glanced at the map. 'That's three minutes we've got to decide how to handle this.'

Another message arrived.

You're late so I've left something there for you.

As Holly relayed the message she felt sickening dread escalate.

'He wants us panicked. Means we'll be off guard,' Maggie placated. 'If he harms Abigail he's given up any hold he has over us.'

'Maybe he's decided he doesn't need it.' Holly could feel the pill sticking in her throat. 'We have little to go to the police with.'

'So why send us to Hexham? He wanted to show us something.'

'Like you said, he probably needed us out of the way while he set up whatever's waiting for us in Brinkley.'

'We have to do as he says. There must be a reason he directed us to the square.' Maggie checked the rear-view.

'I should go in alone.'

'Let's just think about this.'

'No,' Holly said flatly. 'You need to stay out of the way. If he doesn't have the two of us we still have some leverage.'

'That's what we assume.'

'If he ambushes us both there's no negotiation. This way at least I have a shot at getting Abigail back.'

Maggie didn't respond as another gritting truck passed them.

'Drop me off and get parked up somewhere safe.'

CHAPTER FORTY-SIX

Holly took the phone back from Maggie. 'She OK?'

'Sascha's just trying to settle her but Penny knows she's not at home.'

'She's missing you but she's safe.' But Holly didn't know if she could believe her own reassurance. She could see from the satnav that the industrial park was the next left. 'I'll get out here.'

Maggie slowed the car. 'Let's check it out first.'

'No time. Park up way down the road and I'll find you.'

'You can't even call me.'

Holly again regretted stamping on Maggie's cell. 'Anybody stops for you just get the hell out of here. Hiding is the best way you can protect me and Abigail.'

Maggie nodded once. 'Keep your gun at hand.'

'If I'm longer than half an hour take off.'

'Half an hour?'

'Looking at the map it's going to take me a while to cross the park to Lot 4.'

'OK.' Maggie fixed Holly. 'Make it back.'

Holly knew there was nothing more to say. Maggie understood she was her insurance.

Maggie halted the Scion, Holly got out and put her boot into the freezing snow up to her calf. She closed the door behind her and watched Maggie glide by.

Holly jammed one hand in her pocket and pulled down her hood with the other. The wind surged against her, and her coat crackled as she traced the curve of the roadside to the tall sign listing the various businesses that operated out of the park.

Her breathing sounded loud and laboured inside the hood. She passed the expansive Lot 1, which was deserted except for a handful of snowbound cars, and trudged on until she'd cleared the first hexagonal, two-storey warehouse. All the windows were in darkness. The next similar structure was revealed hunkered down in the snow, glowing orange from the streetlights.

Holly momentarily lost the road and waded back out of a drift before turning right and finding a sign for Lots 3 and 4. She trotted down an incline and almost stumbled at the bottom as she hit the lower level. *How many minutes had she taken to get here?* She hoped it had felt longer than it actually was.

She followed the sign for Lot 4 and found the parking bays all empty. But there was a single light on in one of the upper windows. Holly cut across the snow in the lot until she reached a large doorway covered by strips of yellowing transparent plastic.

Was he waiting for her the other side? She was sure his message was a ploy to hide his true intentions. *Or had he really left something for her here?* She wouldn't allow herself to speculate what she could discover.

Holly slipped through the curtain. Warm, metallic-smelling air draped over her. She was standing in a dark loading bay. There was another aroma though. *Food cooking?* Fans pulsed low in the ceiling above. She could make out several forklifts parked up and beyond them were tall rows of packing crates. There was nobody around but there was a steel flight of steps to her left that led to the gantry of the upper floor. Muted light crept halfway down the stairs.

There was a directory sign at the foot of them, and Holly tapped on the flashlight of her phone. As she scanned the words she immediately recognised one of the occupants:

FRESNADE SMOKERY

Holly paused there and looked about her. *Was somebody observing her from the shadows?* To the right of the sign she spotted a rusty green box suspended from a wire. She stretched up to grab it and pushed in one of the oily buttons.

The fan hum got louder so she tried another one. That activated the strip lights, and they flickered on, revealing the enormity of the loading bay and a row of six forklifts parked up to her right. No sign of anybody on the grey concrete floor unless they were skulking in the cubicle office on the far side…

Holly put her foot on the bottom step and paused to listen. There was another noise under the others, which seemed to come from above. A higher pitched whine under the fans and a low occasional thud. Holly slowly climbed, her feet clunking and her heart pumping two beats in between.

When she hit the top she was looking down a gantry with tall shuttered doors leading off it. Only one of them was partially rolled up, and a slice of light from within drew Holly towards it.

It was impossible to approach stealthily as her boots made the whole frame shudder but she reminded herself that she would be foolish to believe she could surprise Babysitter. He'd lured them here, so, if he was waiting, she may as well let him know she'd arrived. As she advanced, the aroma of cooking became stronger. Looked like the smoking was underway. Despite the extractors, the smell of mesquite chips was potent.

She came in line with the open doorway and took in the illuminated interior, which was about forty feet square. A row of eight large stainless steel smoker lockers covered the back wall. Next to them was a walk-in cold storage room. In front of it was a row of wooden prep tables and stacked plastic tubs that looked like they contained large pieces of meat in bright orange marinade. Holly ducked under the door and hastily glanced left and right. Nobody was waiting to pounce on her. She paced slowly towards the prep tables. Large, labelled plastic drums of dry rub were stored under the first, and the thick wooden boards on the second had been wiped down and looked spotless. Nothing had been left for her here.

Something thumped inside one of the smoking lockers, and she swivelled back to the doorway, half expecting to find someone standing there. But she knew she should be able to hear anyone moving along the gantry. Returning her attention to the lockers Holly quickly walked to the middle of the row and tugged the handle of the one immediately in front of her. A blast of heat and smoke escaped, and she squinted against it at what was inside. There were three slowly rotating shelves, and on the first was what looked like a hefty shoulder of pork. She kept the door half closed and watched as another replaced it, then another before the slow revolution brought the original shelf back into view. The thump came again, and she guessed it was coming from the locker next to it. She closed the door and shifted to her left, seizing the handle but not pulling it. The aroma in the room was suddenly overpowering, and her throat tightened. *What was making the noise? Something that had been placed inside that shouldn't be? Something that was too big for the shelf?* Holly gripped the metal hard. *Was she about to be punished for disobeying Babysitter?* She felt dizzy and tensed her stomach as she yanked the door open a crack. Heat escaped with more sickly sweet smoke. Holly let it drop and, as the fumes cleared, saw the side of crusted meat on the shelf immediately in front of her. It rose and dropped out of sight as the next unsteadily ascended. It was heavy, and the bulk of the object slowed the shelf and caught on the lip of the housing as it appeared. It was something wrapped in a pink blanket, and Holly immediately recognised it as Abigail's.

CHAPTER FORTY-SEVEN

Maggie glimpsed the clock on the dash again. Holly had been gone nearly sixteen minutes. But she couldn't go in there to look for her. That was probably exactly what Babysitter wanted and then he'd be able to take care of both of them. *Would he risk harming Holly if he knew Maggie was still able to go to the police? Or was he relying on the fact she wouldn't want to implicate herself?* A movement in her rear-view mirror. Holly was staggering through the snow towards her. As she reached the Scion Maggie leaned over to the passenger side and opened the door. Holly caught it, but didn't get in.

Maggie noticed the fingers holding the hood of Holly's poncho down were a man's a split second before he lunged into the car at her. He seized her hair and yanked it hard towards him, and she cried out as she saw the carving knife in his other hand. She lashed out with her right fist and felt it connect solidly with his face, but his grip didn't loosen as he crawled further over the seat. Maggie tried to block the hand with the blade and it pierced her right palm. He jabbed again at her, but she caught his arm and pushed it down. If she let go to get the gun out of her pocket he'd be able to stab her.

He jerked her head as if he were trying to snap her neck, but Maggie clutched at his Adam's apple with her left fingers.

His right arm trembling against hers, Maggie's attacker lifted the weapon towards her exposed jugular and pressed it against the soft skin there.

Maggie rolled her eyes to him, but the hood had dropped so only his chin was visible.

'See how easy it is?' His voice was clipped and composed. 'I could end this now. Bury you both so nobody will find you. You almost stopped me from driving away with Penny before.'

Icy realisation filtered through her. Maggie dug her nails into his neck, but the action caused the knifepoint to prick her.

'Careful. I'm giving you another chance to keep your daughter safe. Or I can go snatch her now if you want me to.' He dragged her head further back. His breath came in short blasts on her face, warm and sour. 'I just want to show you I can remove you any time I wish. Pop.' His lips puffed saliva onto her cheek. 'I know you'll do anything to preserve the life of your child, Maggie. You could be my quick solution to Holly's disobedience.'

Maggie grunted but remained motionless. It was pointless resisting. He could kill her with only a slight pressure on the blade. 'Where's Holly?'

'Incapacitated.'

'What have you done to her?'

'And to think you tried to kill her only a few hours ago.'

'Where is she?'

'In better condition than you would have left her. But I still want to give you the opportunity to release yourself and Penny. Not now – I need Holly present as well. But you'll soon have to make a choice again. It's always going to be down to that for both of you. But find me and perhaps you'll find Abigail.'

'Let us go. We promise we'll stay silent – you know why.'

'Oh, I know why *you* will. That threat of going to the police had to have come from Holly because I know you can't even consider it.'

Maggie swallowed and the metal stung her again.

'But desperation has made her dangerous too. That's why I believe you both have such great potential.'

'Just let Abigail go.'

'Abigail *may* be released. But that's a decision for later. Perhaps finding who I am, uncovering my story, will help you understand.'

'Whatever we do, you're not going to let us go.' She flinched as his fingers tensed and tugged the roots of her hair.

'I'm a man of my word. Didn't I return Penny to you safe and sound?'

'Before you sent Holly to kill me.'

'The endgame will always be the same. But by not killing you, Holly's chosen a different road for you both.'

'Just let Abigail go.'

'I know I can rely on you, Maggie.'

'Who the fuck are you?'

'Just keep asking that question. And answer it by sunrise. I've left Holly with a clue, but you'll have to go unlock her first.' He took the pressure off the blade and suddenly slid backwards out of the car.

Maggie immediately put her hand on her gun.

Babysitter stood upright in the snow outside. 'If you use that, you may as well be putting a bullet in Abigail's head. You could live with that, could you?'

Maggie could only see the bottom half of Babysitter's face. The man was square-jawed and had thin lips. But it was his nose that was the most recognisable. The flesh between his nostrils was split, like there were two tips. It was definitely the man who had been in Hatchet Park Mall when Penny had been taken.

'She might need this.' He slid off Holly's poncho, balled it up and tossed it in the car. He was wearing a camouflage jacket underneath.

Now she could absorb his face properly, the shadow of dark hair on his shaved head, the thick brows over his hooded eyes and divided nose. He was mid-to late-twenties, of medium build and his body language told her he fully expected her not to pull the gun on him. She did and pointed it directly at his chest. 'I said let her go.'

'Your call, Maggie.' He didn't seem alarmed.

'I mean it.' Her chest heaved. This could be the one chance she had of stopping him. *If she shot Babysitter now would Penny no longer be in danger, or did he have accomplices? But, if she pulled the trigger, he was right about Abigail – how would they ever find her?*

'Tell me where Abigail is.'

He shook his head once. 'She's safe for the moment. But you'd better get going. You know where to find Holly. Better scoot if you still need her to be body temperature.' He slammed the car door but remained where he was.

She could still shoot him through the glass. But he already knew which conclusion she'd come to, and it was pointless delaying it.

Maggie reluctantly started the Scion, turned around and accelerated back towards the industrial park, his figure becoming a green blur before it was swallowed by snow and darkness.

CHAPTER FORTY-EIGHT

Even when Maggie applied the brakes hard, the wheels of the Scion kept sliding down the hill, the whole vehicle slewing sideways before she got traction again and hung a right towards Lot 4.

As she grabbed Holly's coat and got out of the car she could just discern her footprints, their indentations nearly filled in. She followed them. The wind had dropped but the snowfall was still heavy. The crunch of her footfalls echoed off the front of the building, and her breath escaped in huge clouds.

She pushed through the plastic drapes and gazed around the illuminated but deserted loading bay. 'Holly!'

No reply.

A sickly aroma of smoke wafted over her. *Was she too late? Where the hell had Babysitter locked her?* 'Holly!' She peered beyond the forklifts to the tiny office on the far side and strode towards it. 'Holly!'

A muffled yell and pounding from above.

Maggie froze and made for the metal steps to her left. Noticing the name of the smokery she quickly climbed them and thudded noisily along the gantry until she reached the shutter door.

There was frantic banging coming from one of the stainless steel cabinets before her. Maggie ran to them and swiftly swung one open. Nothing inside but cooking chunks of meat.

It came again. *The cold room.* Maggie crossed to it and pressed the button on the handle so it unlocked.

Holly staggered out, arms hugging her body. 'He's here.' She shivered and darted her eyes around.

'No, he's not. He found me.' She handed Holly her coat.

'What happened?' She registered the cut to Maggie's neck. 'He harmed you?'

'I'm OK. He just threatened me.'

'What did he say to you about Abigail?'

'He said she's safe.'

'I have to see her. I have to know she's still alive!'

'Calm down. The situation is the same. He's going to keep her alive, so we do exactly what he wants.'

'You let him go?'

'I had my gun on him but what could I do? If I pulled the trigger we'd never get Abigail back. He told me to release you. Did you find anything here?'

Holly angrily yanked open the door of the smoker behind her.

Through the pungent blue smoke, Maggie could see the doll wrapped in a pink blanket, the middle of its face sucked in by the heat.

'He locked his arm around my neck when I opened it. I blacked out and woke in the cold room. I didn't get a look at his face.' She rubbed her throat.

'I did. He was the guy who snatched Penny from the parking lot. Mid- to late-twenties. Shaved head. Weird splayed nose.'

Holly rubbed the tops of her arms then slid on her coat. 'What did he say to you?'

'That we have to work out who he is by sunrise.'

'What?'

'In other words, we indulge him, go where he tells us. The threat's the same.'

'He had the opportunity to kill both of us.'

Maggie nodded. 'He's enjoying himself. Told me we're to be part of the endgame, and I think it's going to be more fucked up than whatever he originally had planned.'

'So where do we go from here?'

'He said he's already given you a clue.'

Both their eyes slid to the open smoker.

Maggie pulled the doll out. 'Shit!' The blanket was hot, and she dropped it.

The plastic baby rolled face down out of its blanket. Maggie turned it over with her foot so its eyes were looking up at the ceiling, their lids bouncing to a standstill.

They both read what was written on its bare chest.

Waggity Camp Mill

Maggie looked up at Holly. 'Mean anything to you?'

But Holly already had her phone out. She searched for it. 'Waggity Camp. It's a dog kennels in Lime Falls. Run by a Suzanne Welch.'

'How far?'

Holly consulted Google Maps. 'Eleven minutes, probably longer in this weather. We'd better go.' She was already heading for the door.

'Wait. Are we missing something here?' Maggie surveyed the smokery. 'This is Tom Fresnade's old place of work. Shouldn't we be trying to locate his family?'

'Come on, we've got the next destination.'

'So we go running in every direction he sends us?'

'What else can we do if Abigail might be there? We're wasting time.'

Maggie was still reluctant to leave. 'The Fresnades live in town. Shouldn't we call on them?'

'We found Tom Fresnade's name too easily. I think it's going to be more complicated than knocking on their door.'

'But don't you think we should be determining our own direction?'

'No. I can only think of Abigail.'

'Me too.' Maggie could see the anguish on Holly's face, but her instincts told her they needed to consider where they'd just come from. 'Which is why we need to be thinking outside the path Babysitter is leading us down.'

'We know about Fresnade because Babysitter sent us to the square. Maybe we'll discover more if we go to the kennels. Besides, we don't know where the Fresnades live.'

'Check the online directory.'

'We can while we're driving to Lime Falls.' Holly trotted towards the door.

'Which, again, could be a trap.'

She halted. 'Like I said, he could have killed both of us here. This is a journey he wants us alive for.'

'Until the end of it.'

'Sounds like he has it all planned out, but we don't have much time left and the police are still looking for us.'

Maggie took a breath. 'OK. Lime Falls. Wait a moment.' She carefully picked up the doll with the hot blanket. 'Maybe this is more than a pointer. Let's take it with us.' She wrapped it and walked out onto the gantry.

Holly was ahead. 'Ever been to Lime Falls?'

'No. You?'

Holly didn't answer until they'd reached the top of the steps. 'Once.'

FORTY-NINE

Holly started shivering uncontrollably in the car. She registered the pain at her hip had subsided. But Sascha's pill was making her feel dislocated, as if she had to focus hard on her surroundings. *Or was it because she was still groggy after Babysitter's attack?* Her throat felt bruised.

Maggie started the engine and turned on the heating again. 'So when did you visit Lime Falls?'

'My ex took me hiking there. Long time ago.'

Maggie accelerated across the lot to the exit side. 'Your ex, as in Abigail's father?'

'No. Before Adam. I'm talking six years ago. Patrick Dundas. But he also took me to Hexham.' It had occurred to her as soon as she'd found the address for Waggity Camp. 'But it seems like such a long time ago.'

'Patrick Dundas?' Maggie accelerated the Scion back up the incline.

They both held their breath as the wheels struggled, but Maggie floored it and they levelled off.

'He was how I met Adam. They were best friends. I dated Patrick for about a year but we both knew it wasn't going anywhere. We called it a day and that's when I hooked up with Adam. Adam always made me laugh.' Life had seemed so uncomplicated to Holly then.

'His best friend. How was Patrick with that?'

'He was already dating somebody else by then, Lily Marchant. They got married a couple of years later.'

'So what happened with Adam?'

'He passed away,' Holly stated, stoically.

Maggie's eyes darted. 'I'm sorry.'

But Holly could tell she was too busy turning over the facts in her head.

'When?'

'Five months before Abigail was born.' She didn't wait for Maggie to ask the next obvious question. 'Aneurysm. In a gas station forecourt when he was filling the car. I wasn't with him.'

'That's tough.' Maggie negotiated the car past the first building. 'So that was only, what?'

'Just over two years ago.' She still couldn't believe there had already been two anniversaries of his death.

'So was he still in touch with Patrick?'

'Just the occasional text. Patrick moved to South Dakota. Look, I think it's a bit of a stretch that Patrick may be part of this. I went to Hexham a few times but not always with him.'

'We can't dismiss anyone.' Maggie leaned against the wheel and peered through the snow. 'There's the entrance.'

'I agree. So what about your ex?' Holly knew there was no time for sensitivity.

'Jeff? He wouldn't want to stalk me. He's all about running away as far as he can.'

'Where is he now?'

'Don't know. He had a sister in Gainesville.'

'When did he leave you?'

'Last year. Two days after my diagnosis. Perhaps he thought that was a respectable enough interval.'

'Asshole.'

Maggie pulled them into the road and followed the satnav towards Lime Falls. 'I wish I could dismiss him as easily. But I knew who he was when I took him on. Jeff was a damaged person. He was commitment phobic but not for the usual reasons. He lost his brother then his parents within about a year.'

'Jesus.'

'His brother was the golden boy. Committed suicide. He had older infirm parents and that seemed to finish them both. He didn't want to get close to anyone after that, so it was a miracle he wanted to move in with me. I pressured him though. He almost hightailed it when I got pregnant. I didn't think my cancer would be the last nail in someone else's coffin.'

'Coward.'

'Yes. What's happening now, he wouldn't be able to deal with it. But he couldn't be part of this.'

Holly took out the phone and opened Google.

'What are you looking for?'

'The Fresnades' address. I'm going to see if I can find Rich Temple as well.'

'The guy whose daughter drowned?'

'Yeah. And maybe the daughter who survived still lives locally.'

'What was her name?'

'Colette.' Holly was already scanning the online directory. 'A couple of Richard Temples but only one Colette Temple.'

'Where does she live?'

'Larch Grove.'

'Where the hell's that?'

'Just outside Crystal Bay.'

'That's a long drive. And we're gonna need gas soon.' Maggie glanced at the dash.

Holly regarded the needle. They were nearly empty.

CHAPTER FIFTY

'Do you consider yourself a good mother?' Maggie eyed the gas gauge again.

'I cope.'

'That's not what I asked.'

'Yes. I believe I am,' Holly replied earnestly. 'Why?'

'I just wonder if we're being punished. For being single mothers.'

'Didn't Janet Braun have a partner?'

Maggie had forgotten she'd given Holly that impression. 'She was sleeping with someone, but her Facebook page said she was single.'

'So you think Babysitter is some kind of single-mother-hating religious freak or something?'

'Just trying to work out why he would target us.'

Holly's expression hardened. 'Let people judge after they've tried to bring up a child on their own.'

Maggie nodded. 'Every time I switch the light off in Penny's nursery is like a victory. Sometimes it scares me it's my responsibility alone to want the best for her. But that gives me clarity. It's terrifying but it makes me happy. Now, I don't think I'd want it any other way.'

Holly inhaled. 'Every morning I set my alarm five minutes early. In that time I have to fill myself up, make myself strong for Abigail before I even get out of bed. I'll never forgive myself for allowing her to be taken.'

'He would have found a way no matter how vigilant you were. No need for self-recrimination. Just concentrate on getting her back.'

*

They reached Lime Falls before they found a gas station. The dash alert told Maggie they'd have to get to one soon. She usually got a good few miles on reserve, but driving through the snow was burning more fuel.

Drifts clogged the narrow route into the tiny community. There were no streetlights, but a long row of houses decorated with blue fairy lights allowed her to trace the camber of the road.

'The satnav says this is it.' Holly peered into the shadows beside her.

'There.' Maggie's headlights illuminated the wooden sign to their right. She could just make out the lower part of 'Waggity Camp' through the snow that had been blown against it. 'Shit, another hill.' She swung the car towards the dark opening in the trees, had second thoughts and reversed towards the houses. 'Let's take a run at it.'

Jamming her foot on the pedal she rocketed them up the incline, but they started rolling down. She slammed on the brakes, and the Scion slid backwards. They settled at the bottom again, lodging in a drift behind them.

She killed the engine. 'Let's go on foot. It can't be that far.' Maggie examined the single set of tyre tracks she'd left in the snow before them. 'No other vehicles have been through here recently.'

'Doesn't mean he's not up there.' Holly opened her door and swung herself out.

As they walked under the tree cover every crunch they made seemed magnified by the branches above.

Soon the slope made the backs of Maggie's legs pound, and they were both wheezing for breath.

'I can see a light on up there.'

Maggie followed Holly's gaze to a small glow ahead of them. She loosened the collar of her coat.

They were now on open ground and dogs started barking. Sounded like there were a lot of them.

'I'm not big on dogs.' But Holly didn't slow her pace.

'They're all probably locked up.'

'We don't know that for sure.'

'Don't worry. I grew up around them,' Maggie placated, although the aggression in the cacophony unsettled her.

'Well, whoever owns this place knows we're coming.'

The barking intensified as the outline of a lone, two-storey house emerged against the moonlight. Maggie could make out a tall boundary wall at the left side of it. On the other was an area surrounded by a tall fence, dark canine shapes moving within it as they noisily anticipated their arrival.

'Are they all the right side of the wire?' Holly observed them nervously.

'Looks like it.' There were about eight to ten dogs snapping their jaws at the women and pacing the perimeter.

Their attention was drawn to an outside light coming on beside the front door of the house. It opened, and an obese man was standing in the frame aiming a double-barrelled shotgun at them.

'Who the fuck are you two?' His voice was dried out and mean.

Maggie halted and gripped Holly's coat to prevent her from continuing further. 'It's OK!'

'What's OK, that you're trespassing or that you're doing it in the early hours of the morning?' He rounded on the dogs. 'Shut the fuck up!'

They didn't obey.

'Our car broke down at the bottom of the hill. We're out of gas,' Maggie improvised.

'And why's that my problem?'

'I'm Mrs Johnson.' Maggie said it as if he should recognise her.

'Who?'

Maggie was sure the deceit was going to backfire before she'd started. 'I live in Brinkley. You have my dogs here twice a year.'

He frowned.

'I know that doesn't give me a right to impose but this is the only place I know in Lime Falls.'

'OK.' But he sounded uncertain. 'Johnson?'

'Yeah. I was going to give you a call later this month. I'm in Hawaii for Christmas.'

'Suzy handles all that side of the business.' He lowered the gun. 'Why didn't you phone ahead?'

'My cell's died. We're sorry to scare you like this. Is Suzy there?'

'No, she's visiting with her sister.'

Maggie tried not to show her relief. Was her bluff going to hold up?

'You'd better come in a minute,' he conceded grudgingly. 'Shut the fuck up!' he yelled again.

'What the hell are those dogs doing out in this weather?' Holly whispered.

Maggie moved forward and gestured her to follow.

The dogs snarled as they skirted the fence. He monitored their approach but didn't step back from the doorway.

'What are you out this time of night for anyway?'

Maggie could see his piggy features were still suspicious. He looked to be in his fifties and had short thinning silver hair and stubble. 'I was taking my friend to the hospital.'

His scrutiny lingered on Holly. 'What's wrong with her?' he asked as if she couldn't answer for herself.

'I'm anaemic,' Holly answered immediately.

'Got plenty of red meat for the dogs.' He showed her his uneven teeth and flattened his back to the edge of the doorframe so they could step through.

Because of his build there was hardly any space so they both had to brush past him.

Maggie turned when she heard the door close. They were in a dingy narrow hallway, and there was the strong aroma of dogs and stale cooked onions.

'Phone's right in there.' The man gestured to the closed door on their right.

Maggie felt a surge of panic. She'd been so concerned about her own lies being accepted that she hadn't considered he might be telling his own. After all, Babysitter had sent them there.

Holly pushed the door, and there was darkness the other side. 'Can you switch on the light for us?' She obviously shared Maggie's hesitancy.

The man sighed and lumbered to where they were standing. He leaned through and flicked it.

The old paper shade cast a yellow glow over the small, shabby lounge. There were two armchairs, a couch, a TV, and a coffee table. On it was a red phone positioned next to a hinged open and empty pizza box.

'Knock yourself out. You want me to see if I can scare you up some gas?'

'We'd really appreciate it.' Holly smiled.

'OK, I'll see what I got in the trucks.' He shuffled by them and headed towards a sealed door at the end of the hall.

They both watched him reach it and then disappear through. They glimpsed a lit kitchen the other side before the door swung back into place.

Maggie stared fixedly at it. 'There's something not right.'

'We should take a look around while he's out there.' Holly entered the tiny lounge and took it in.

'Wait—' Maggie hissed.

There was the squeal of a rear screen door opening and closing.

'OK.' Maggie joined her.

'I don't even know what we're looking for.' Holly inspected the walls.

There were a few prints in small frames but nothing else.

Maggie picked up the phone for appearances' sake. 'I've got a bad feeling about this.'

'I think he swallowed your story.'

'Maybe. But he doesn't strike me as the sort of guy to give away free gas.' Maggie got no tone. 'This is dead.' She checked the wire leading to the wall and saw it had been unplugged.

There was a clicking sound in the hallway and they both glanced back to the doorway. A squat, light tan pit bull with brown spots around its pink mouth was standing there, its ears raised and wet fur glistening with fresh snowflakes.

'Hello, boy,' Holly murmured apprehensively.

The dog cocked its head and padded a foot over the threshold.

Maggie tensed and put down the phone. She knew the breed. And suspected their host had just let it in from the yard. 'Move behind the couch. Slowly.' She put her hand on the gun in her pocket, and the dog's lip lifted as it started growling.

Two more older pit bulls appeared behind it, their fur darker but the hostility in their black eyes no less focussed.

CHAPTER FIFTY-ONE

One of them licked at the snowflakes on its snout with its pink tongue. Their throats buzzed in unison before the first barked harshly.

Maggie briefly checked on Holly. She'd taken a few paces back to the couch. 'Slowly.'

The first dog darted forward and snarled at Maggie.

'Stay!' she snapped.

But the dog lunged, its teeth piercing her jeans and clamping onto the flesh above her left knee. She yelled and instinctively struck the top of its warm, wet skull with her fist, but it didn't release her.

Maggie pulled out her snubbie and fired it into the ceiling. Plaster dust puffed over her as the reverberation pushed the sound out of her right ear.

Two of the dogs ran from the room, but the one at her leg held on.

'I'll shoot them all!' Maggie shouted to the man she assumed was hiding in the kitchen. Her voice was deafening in her head.

The other two dogs immediately re-entered the lounge and were joined by another. They made a beeline to where Holly was standing behind the couch.

'Shoot them!' But despite the dog's teeth fastening tighter Maggie hesitated as she pointed her weapon. She trained the barrel beside its ear and fired at the floor.

The dog flinched but still didn't let go.

She heard a shot from behind her and a canine howl. Two of the dogs scampered out of the room again but the agony as the dog chewed at her meant she could only focus on making it stop. She put the barrel against its cranium.

A movement in front of her.

Maggie looked up and saw the obese man enter with his double-barrelled shotgun and point it at her face.

But the discharge came from behind her.

The man's shoulder whipped back, and he cried out. His face was mortified as he slumped against the doorframe. 'Fucking… bitch.'

Briefly, the whole room came to a standstill, but then the pain kicked back in. Maggie looked down and saw the dog gazing up at her, her blood all around its jaws. It had let go and turned to its master.

The man bent over and dropped to his knees. 'Jesus.' He hinged slowly forward until his face was against the floorboards.

The pit bull scuttled to him, nudging its head against his.

Maggie glimpsed Holly standing with her Browning still pointed. Her face was set in an expression of revulsion. Another dog was cowering in the corner, one of its ears bloody and ragged from the first shot Holly had fired.

'Is he dead?' Holly kept the gun on him, her hand trembling.

'No, I'm fucking not!' he gasped. 'Get off.' He swiped at the first dog with his arm, and it vaulted him to join the others outside.

Maggie rushed forward and snatched the shotgun from his grip. He didn't put up any resistance. She could see Holly's bullet had taken a chunk out of his shoulder. 'You clipped him.'

'Call me an ambulance,' he said to the floor.

Maggie pocketed her snubbie and hefted the shotgun. It felt so heavy. 'I got both barrels aimed at your head.' She shakily directed it at the rug though. She didn't want to even risk it going off at him. 'You OK, Holly?'

'No,' Holly eventually replied.

'You injured?'

'No.'

Maggie knew Holly was in shock. 'Come stand next to me.'
Maggie didn't shift her attention from the wounded man. The dog
in the corner growled low as she heard Holly's footfalls approach
but it was more a grumble of pain. Out of the side of her eye she
could see Holly's trembling hand holding her Browning; she put her
fingers on the barrel and pushed it down. Maggie didn't want her
pulling the trigger again by mistake. 'Why did you try to kill us?'

'Call me a fucking ambulance!'

The other dog sloped out of the room.

'Not until you tell me.'

'I'm bleeding out.'

Maggie looked beyond him. She could hear the dogs scratching
about in the hallway. 'Call them off.'

He coughed harshly at the floor.

'If they come through that door again, I'll use your shotgun
and you're likely to get some as well.'

'I can't call them off.'

'Then crawl forward towards me, slowly.'

He groaned as he lugged his heavy frame.

Maggie nodded at Holly, and she quickly slammed the door
and returned to her position beside her. 'Who are you?'

'You already know that. And I know my rights.'

Maggie exchanged a confused glance with Holly. 'We're not
cops.'

'Yeah, right.'

'Sooner you answer the question the sooner you'll get medical
treatment.'

'You can't do that,' he exclaimed indignantly.

'Name.' Maggie could feel the exposed bite burning.

'Connor Welch.'

'Suzanne's husband?'

'Brother.' He squeezed out a low moan.

'Why did you try to kill us?'

'You gonna let me die in front of you?' His voice was suddenly feeble.

Was it an act? 'You'd be surprised what we're capable of. It's your choice. We can plug the phone back in and get you a medic or we can sit this out.'

'Phone rang twenty minutes before you arrived. Guy said… said you were undercover cops.'

'We're not cops.'

'Who the fuck are you then?'

'Tell us which guy.'

'Don't know. Just said it was a friendly warning,' he croaked. 'That I should be prepared.'

'So what have you got to hide from the police?'

He didn't answer.

CHAPTER FIFTY-TWO

Holly's ear felt like it was filling with warm water, and the tone of the gunfire hiss changed as it did. She'd shot someone. When she set out that evening she thought she wasn't capable of it. Now she'd pulled the trigger defending the person she was meant to have killed.

'The cops will be all over this place if I ring you an ambulance.' Maggie sucked air in through her teeth and readjusted the weight on her injured left leg.

'I don't give a shit about that. Just get me a medic.' Connor raised his head, but dropped it to the floorboards again. 'I think I'm… think I'm gonna pass out.'

Maggie examined the blood spots around the punctures in her jeans. 'Tell us what you had to hide from the police.'

'Jesus… just help me.' Pain pinched his words.

'What's Waggity Camp Mill?' Maggie asked sternly.

'I just let them use the place. Nothing to do with me.'

'Who?' Maggie demanded.

'Don't know what they get up to in there and don't want to. They're people you really don't want to fuck with,' he slurred at the floor.

'We'll make that decision. Tell us where it is.' Maggie nodded at the phone on the coffee table.

The handset was off the hook.

Holly replaced it and picked up the whole unit.

'Out back. Down the slope to the river.'

Maggie continued the interrogation. 'What do we find there?'

'They keep it locked.'

'Who?'

'I don't know who. I deal with one guy.' His breathing was laboured. 'Don't know his name. He pays me to let them use it. I make sure it stays private. That's the deal. Only met him once. Money turns up in my account every six months.'

'Is he the one who called you?'

'Didn't say it was. Could have been,' he responded weakly.

Holly gripped the phone tight. She had to get him help.

'How far is the mill, Connor?'

He was motionless.

There was blood pooling around his shoulder and Holly was relieved he was still breathing. She lifted the handset from the cradle.

Maggie held up her palm. 'Wait. Connor? We're not going to dial until you tell us exactly where it is.'

He still didn't reply.

Maggie shook her head. 'We need to see the mill.'

'But he could be bleeding to death.'

'He tried to kill us. And he could be faking,' Maggie said aloud. 'One of us could stay here and keep a gun on him while the other has a scout around.'

Holly didn't look up from Connor's prostrate form. 'How long d'you think the ambulance will take to get here?'

'In this weather, could be half an hour.'

'Might be long enough for me to find the mill. You dress your wound.'

'We don't know how many acres this property sits on.'

'I'll call 911. Then I'll go hunt for it.' Holly could tell Maggie was genuinely prepared to withhold the ambulance. 'If I can't find it in fifteen minutes we'll have to split.'

'OK, fine, but you'd better hurry.' Maggie kept her attention on Connor.

Holly lifted the red handset, but there was no tone. She fumbled the wire into the wall and dialled.

'Which service?' the female operator sounded bored.

'Ambulance. A man's been shot.' Holly knew that would immediately be flagged to the police.

'Putting you through.'

Holly quickly relayed their location to the next voice before hanging up on them.

'You'd better get moving.' Maggie adjusted her grip on the shotgun. 'I'll stay with him for now, but I'll meet you back at the car.'

Holly set the phone on the coffee table and headed for the door.

'Careful,' Maggie cautioned.

She stepped wide of Connor and listened at the panel. No dog activity outside, but that didn't mean she wouldn't get pounced on as soon as she walked into the hallway. Holly took a deep breath and half opened it.

There were no pit bulls in sight. She inched out. None by the front entrance, but the back door was ajar. She let the one behind her close, padded to the kitchen and sealed it.

'You OK?' Maggie called.

'So far. Gonna check upstairs.'

She ascended them, Browning extended and her hip smarting as she reached the top. There were five frowsy rooms, and she swiftly investigated each, turning the light on and then closing the door – bathroom, three bedrooms and an office. Nobody. If any of the dogs were cowering up here she'd shut them in.

Returning to the hallway she made her way to the kitchen door and listened. She could hear panting. Holly gently pushed the panel and found the pit bull with the injured ear lying in front of the sink unit. Blood was smeared around the tiles. Its tongue was hanging out but, although it cocked its head and studied her, it made no move to attack.

Holly's gaze settled on the open back door to her right.

A dog barked from beyond it. *Should she go out through the front entrance and down the side of the property?* But she might not be able to access the rear from the other side of the perimeter wall.

The injured dog didn't move. Holly clocked the faded photograph on the refrigerator. It was Connor kneeling beside a woman in a wheelchair. There was a wooden shield of hooks with keys hanging from them on the wall beside it.

She eased herself around the door. The dog didn't budge. Holding her breath, she hastily snatched up each fob off the hooks and slipped into the yard, pulling the door closed behind her.

Something scurried in the darkness to her right, and she followed the noise with her barrel until she spotted the metal gate before her. Holly hurried through it and slammed it shut.

A bright light came on illuminating the snowflakes drifting in the space around her. She whirled around and found it was a movement detector light mounted on the front of the wooden roof of the lean-to she'd just walked out of.

Holly was standing in an ivy walled courtyard surrounded by metal cages. They were all empty.

Barking started in earnest again, and she could discern the shapes of the dogs behind the wire fence that divided the kennels from what she guessed was the exercise yard. She was relieved to be the right side of it.

On the far left of the courtyard a door was set into the wall. *Did that lead to the grounds at the rear of the property?* She hurriedly trudged through the snow and undid the icy latch.

CHAPTER FIFTY-THREE

Maggie sat on the arm of the couch and took the pressure off the dog bite. 'She's gone now. There's nobody here you can fool.' She was convinced Connor was faking.

He remained silent.

'Cops'll be here soon. Before we split, I could call them, tell them to take a look at this mill. Not the sort of attention the people who use it would want. And where will that leave you? Or you can just tell me everything you know about it now and we'll leave you to make up whatever story you like about intruders.'

He still said nothing.

'OK.' Maggie picked up the phone from the coffee table with her left hand and dialled.

'I told you all I know,' he replied gutturally.

'Thought you were still conscious.' She tried not to let her relief register. 'Where is it?' Maggie replaced the receiver and supported the barrels so they were pointing at the door above him. The weapon made her nervous, and she didn't trust it not to go off.

'She'll find it. But they keep it locked up.' He shifted.

'Just keep your face against the floor. Where's the key?'

'Don't have one. And I really don't know what they use it for.'

'Bullshit.' She lightly gripped her wound and cringed as it sent an aftershock of pain along her leg.

'I don't ask any questions.'

'Your sister part of this?'

'Suzy's in a wheelchair; she can't get down the slope.'

'What do they do out there?'

'Told you I don't know. They use the waterway. Never come by here.'

'I'll let the police work it out then.' Maggie lifted the receiver again.

'Stop! Jesus.'

'In your own time.'

'OK… OK.' He settled on a response. 'I saw them down there one night. Three of them coming in on a boat.' He grunted. 'Two guys and a girl. She had tape around her face. Hands tied behind her back.'

'What happened?'

'They walked her inside the mill. Lights came on for a while. And then they left. Just the two of them.'

'What about the girl?'

'I hung around.' He tried to fill his lungs but winced. 'She didn't come out of there.'

'So you didn't go down there, even though they'd left?'

'No.'

'OK, I'll let the cops know you'll finish the story up for them.'

'It was locked.'

'What are they hiding? You must know.'

'I swear I don't. It's their business. I don't want to know.'

Maggie stood and sucked in a breath. It felt like the dog's teeth were still biting her. 'Didn't you try to get to the girl?'

'Sure. I wanted to see she was OK.'

'Yeah, right.' She imagined what would have happened if he'd got past the door and she was still tied up.

'I knocked, tried to get a response. Nothing.'

'And when you didn't, the next thing you did was call the cops.'

Connor didn't answer.

Maggie was repulsed. He'd stood around while the girl had been abused or even worse and stayed silent. What else had he turned a blind eye to? 'And that's the only time you ever saw anybody?'

'Yes.'

'What really happened?'

'That's the truth. I hear things but I don't go near there now.'

'You said they're people we really don't want to fuck with. So you must know more about them than you're letting on.'

'I don't. If you saw what they did to that girl you would have come to the same conclusion.'

'But you said you didn't see what they did to her.'

Connor began breathing erratically.

'Save it.'

It eventually subsided. 'She didn't come out of there. That's all I know.'

Maggie was positive he knew a whole lot more. 'How do you contact them?'

'I don't. Money goes into my account.'

'What do you know about Babysitter?'

'I don't know what you're talking about.'

She believed him. *If Babysitter was party to what went on at the mill why would he send them there? Did he think Connor would finish them off? But Babysitter could have killed them himself already.* 'What about the names Tom Fresnade or Rich Temple?'

'No.'

'Think hard.'

'I don't fucking know them, OK?'

Whatever the connection was, Babysitter was lurking somewhere in between but, with time running out before the police arrived, they had to make themselves scarce. The car was still parked at the bottom of the hill, and the cops would be looking for their licence plate. 'I've still got the shotgun pointing at your head.'

He cowered, covering it with both hands.

Maggie tugged on the phone. The wire tensed and popped out of the wall socket. She kept the unit in her hand and limped quickly to the door. She didn't want Connor calling anyone, especially his friends from the mill. 'Try anything and I'll use it.'

'So you're really not cops?' he rasped against the floor.

'Just wait for the ambulance.'

'Then you're in a whole heap of shit now.' Connor seemed amused.

'We might not be done with you yet.'

No dogs in the hall. Maggie pulled the door behind her and quickly made for the front entrance.

Outside she stopped and cast her eyes around the front yard at the white domes of covered bushes. The dogs started barking at her through the fence again. *Were they getting the scent of her blood? Was Babysitter watching nearby?* Maggie tossed the phone.

She hoped Holly had found the mill and was on her way back. If Connor's story was to be believed there was no way she was getting inside.

She hobbled back down the hill, gripping bush branches tightly to stop her falling headfirst. When she hit the bottom she got in the car and quickly reversed it to the end of the row of houses and tucked it around the corner.

Maggie switched off the engine. The only sound was her panting and the fizz of gunfire in her right ear. Her leg throbbed in time with her heartbeat. Through the condensation on the glass she could see both ways along the road. No sign of the ambulance.

She slid the shotgun onto the back seat. Holly had better move her ass. They were cutting it fine.

CHAPTER FIFTY-FOUR

Holly had spotted the mill and, pocketing her Browning and the keys, concentrated on keeping her balance as she weaved her way through the glowing snow-capped rocks that littered the incline that led to it. The sturdy grey brick structure was perched on a bend in a narrow waterway that looked pitch-black between its white banks. There were no lights on in the tiny slit windows of the little building, and a thick bonnet of moon-soaked snow seemed poised to tumble from its apex roof.

She knew the trauma of shooting Connor hadn't even begun to play catch-up. How many minutes had it taken her to get down here? She checked her watch.

4:46 a.m.

Just over two hours until sunrise.

Babysitter had specified the mill. She had to at least attempt to open the door.

She hit the bottom of the slope and had about another thirty feet to cover before she reached it. After several paces she was just fumbling for her phone flashlight when Holly plunged into deep snow. It was over her head, in her mouth, and all she could hear was her own frantic breathing. She slid further down. Her feet still hadn't touched the ground.

There was no point yelling. Nobody was around to hear. She squinted at the inky sky through the hole above her, but couldn't lift her arms from her sides. The snow was too tightly packed around her. Holly waggled herself and dropped another few inches before the soles of her boots made contact with soft mud. And she was sinking into it.

Holly told herself to stay calm and stop struggling. She slowed her breathing, but could barely fill her lungs because of the pressure of the snow. If she didn't show up at the car, Maggie would come. Holly sank further and felt the wet cold clamp her ankles. *But would she find her in time?*

She couldn't afford to be stuck. For Abigail's sake. *Think.* There was no one she could call, even if she could reach her phone. *What was her best way out?* If she could just get one arm free. *But if she did might she slide deeper down?*

There was no time to deliberate. And no other options she could think of. Grunting, she slowly drew her right arm past her constricted body, but couldn't bend it sufficiently to get her hand to her chest. She made short sharp jabs with her right elbow against the wall and started carving a small hollow.

After a few minutes she had enough space to manoeuvre, and bent her arm. Holly got her right hand to her chin before extending it upwards.

As she grasped the looser snow above she slithered another inch down. She maintained her hold though, digging her fingers in hard to lodge herself in position before slamming her frame sideways and getting her other arm up and free.

She dug in the fingers of her left hand, felt her stomach muscles fluttering as they took her weight, and groaned as her bullet wound reminded her of its presence.

Holly had never had much upper-arm strength. Could never handle the monkey bars. But she knew if she let go now she probably wouldn't be able to clamber back up again. She thought of her daughter, tautened her abdomen and tried to pull her boots out of the swamp.

Her fingers already felt numb and wouldn't be able to maintain a hold on the powdery snow for long. Cursing through her gritted teeth she hauled her bulk up and felt her feet breaking contact with the mud. She couldn't allow herself to slip back.

Holly trembled and squirmed upwards, thrusting herself towards the sky before embedding her right hand a few inches higher in the snow. She had to keep going, repositioned her left above that and opened her freed legs against the sides to keep her in place.

She could see the edge of the hole; feel the fresh air against her face. She screamed and boosted herself forward, clawing with both hands as she heaved herself out.

Holly hoisted her legs clear and propelled herself backwards on her buttocks to the bottom of the incline. Panting, she took in the shape of the basin. There was higher ground to the right of it.

She got to her feet, her escape already forgotten. *Should she still risk investigating the mill, or head straight back to the car?*

CHAPTER FIFTY-FIVE

Holly used the flashlight of her phone to make her way tentatively towards the bank, the beam illuminating the snowfall in front of her. She tested each pace forward before putting pressure on her boot. Sticking to the ridge she was soon at the water. The entrance of the mill faced the river.

She found a small flight of steps that were buried in snow and used the toe of her boot to feel the edge of each one and ascend to a recessed wooden door. The lock was a modern one, and she fumbled out the keys she'd taken from the kitchen and tried each one.

Three of the eleven keys slid into the lock. But they wouldn't turn. She was wasting time and would probably have to slip by police to get back to the car. *Was there really something inside that Babysitter wanted them to find? Or had he called Connor to warn him of their arrival?*

But now she was here Holly had to try and gain entry, otherwise she wouldn't know if she'd missed something vital. She decided to insert the three keys again, and twist them harder. *Maybe the lock was frozen.*

The second one made a snap sound, and Holly thought she'd broken it, but the door suddenly relaxed from the frame.

Holly pushed on the heavy panel, and it swung into a dim stone passage. She tensed and stepped inside. The door gently glided shut behind her. It felt colder than outside.

The beam picked up three doorless rooms, one to her left, right and straight ahead. Over the musty aroma of aged and rotten wood there was another, more artificial, scent. A cloying air freshener that smelt of sickly, synthetic lemon.

She stopped at the aperture to her left. Inside she could see the remnants of the mill workings, its mechanics rusted and its flat, circular grinding stones shrouded by leaves and cobwebs.

She cautiously moved to the next empty chamber. The floor was covered by a square of grubby fawn carpet, and there were dark stains near the rear wall below the slit window. She played the beam over them. It appeared to be blood but there was something else scattered there.

She entered to get a closer look, and they glinted in the flashlight. Fragments of teeth.

Holly backed from the room. There was no way of imprisoning somebody inside it but that made the discovery even more repellent. Once the front door of the mill was locked there was no escape.

She shone the flashlight to the end doorway but the light couldn't reach far enough to penetrate its dark interior. That was where the potent air freshener smell emanated from. Another wave of it rolled out at her. Every particle of her wanted to turn and flee.

Holly tried to swallow, once, twice but it felt as if her dread was a solid lump in her throat. She couldn't walk out without glimpsing what was inside the room, however, and advanced, her beam extending into its blackness.

A rustle halted her in her tracks.

Sounded like a plastic bag. She waited. 'Hello?' Her voice was dampened by the low ceiling.

Nothing.

The air freshener was overpowering, and she could taste its acrid sweetness at the back of her tongue. 'Hello?' She swung the phone rapidly around the granite bricks of the inner walls, and it shifted the shadows of something that was piled on the floor. Holly padded forward and directed the flashlight downwards.

There were a number of garbage bags there. She reached the doorway and played it along the nearest until she caught a man's face staring back at her.

The whites of his eyes glinted behind thin orange polythene, and Holly recoiled. But the spotlight remained on his moustachioed face and half-open mouth.

Holly's hand was over her own.

The rustle came again, and she froze.

But she could see the man hadn't moved. His skin was mottled, his collapsed expression unblinking. *Was there somebody else alive in there?*

There was motion beyond the dead man. Polythene shifting.

'Answer me if you need help.'

The man's face was silent but now Holly could distinguish the blue torso of the corpse behind him. *How many bodies? Five, six?*

The disturbance intensified, and the source of the noise sprang up. A rat scuttled over the cadavers from the rear of the room and was quickly followed by a stream of others.

Holly turned and ran, her beam swivelling from the silver flashes in their eyes.

CHAPTER FIFTY-SIX

From the car, Maggie had watched the ambulance make three attempts to climb the hill to the kennels before sliding back down. The paramedics unloaded their kit and were about to ascend on foot when a patrol car arrived and two officers got out and had a confab with them. The snow was still falling heavily.

The four of them clambered the incline, and Maggie hoped Holly wasn't coming the other way.

A couple of lights came on in the row of houses she was parked beside and lit up the scene. People were getting curious about the emergency vehicles. *Come on, Holly.* Soon they'd be coming out to investigate. *Was Babysitter observing them?* No sign of his Nissan pickup.

Maggie prayed Penny was obliviously sleeping at Sascha's by now.

Had something happened at the mill? Should she sneak by while they were attending to Connor? Maggie was about to open her door when Holly slid down and into view.

She halted and looked frantically around. Maggie flashed her headlights once. She awkwardly sprinted to where she was parked and got into the passenger seat. Maggie started the engine.

'Anything?' She didn't even wait for Holly to close the door before she pulled out.

'Bodies.'

'What?' Maggie turned to Holly's sickened features.

'Five or six in there.'

'Jesus.'

'Wrapped in polythene.'

Maggie could see how shaken Holly was. 'How did you get in?'

'There was a bunch of keys in the kitchen.'

'Son of a bitch.' Maggie drove slowly out of Lime Falls. She was tempted to floor it, but didn't want to call any unwanted attention to them. She sucked in air through her teeth as her bite pulsed under her jeans.

'You OK?'

Maggie nodded.

'You *should* get that dressed.' It was a declaration not a suggestion. 'How about a Demerol?' Holly looked in the glove box for the pills.

'Already taken one.' Maggie massaged the area above the wound. 'Connor said he didn't *have* a key. Gave me some story about other guys showing up on a boat and dragging a girl in there.'

'He knows much more than he's told us.' Holly closed the glove box but shook the pills.

Maggie picked up speed as they entered the woods again. 'Well Connor's no use to us now. He's going to be talking to the cops for the foreseeable.'

'Maybe we should call them and report what I found in there.'

'Agreed. But not just yet. Let's see if there's anything online about Connor. What was the surname?'

'Welch.' Holly was already entering it into her phone.

'Can't be too many of them locally. We've really got to get gas.'

'Found a news story.' Holly hit the results.

'Well?'

'Arrested in 2011. Attacked an elderly woman in her front yard with a fence post. Sentenced to five years in Hubbard Penitentiary.'

'Nice guy. Anything else?'

'Looks like that took him off the scene for a while.'

'What about his sister?' Maggie waited while she searched.

'Suzanne Welch. This looks like her.' Holly tapped the screen. '"Doggie Fun Day Fund Raiser. Local kennel owner Suzanne Welch raised over seven hundred dollars for cerebral palsy charity Mindset and said she was happy to increase awareness of the condition and was planning to hold another similar event if her health allowed."'

'Polar opposite. When was that?'

'Last July.'

Maggie watched Lime Falls receding in her mirror. 'But are these people relevant to Babysitter, or was he just trying to direct us to the mill?'

'So Connor said he had nothing to do with it?'

'Claims he's just a janitor, but if he has a key…'

'Maybe he works for Babysitter, and he's implicating us so we can never go to the police.' Holly put on her belt.

Maggie hadn't considered that. She wondered if Babysitter was building a story with their fingerprints all over it.

'But what has any of this got to do with Tom Fresnade or Rich Temple?'

'Perhaps nothing. Maybe our focus should be the locations he's sent us to instead of people.'

'But he's told us to work out who he is.' Holly rattled the bottle again and seemed to be thinking about taking another Demerol.

Her phone buzzed. Holly checked the display. 'Phone call. Don't recognise the number. Sascha?' She answered nervously. 'Hello?'

Maggie shot her eyes to the road and back to Holly's wary expression.

CHAPTER FIFTY-SEVEN

'I hope Connor extended you every hospitality.'

It was the first time Holly had heard Babysitter's voice. It was calm and contained. 'We've done what you asked. Give me my daughter.'

'You're two very resourceful women. To walk out of there you must be.'

'Did you call ahead and tell him we were cops?'

'That's the only reason he didn't kill you. Two bodies he couldn't have quietly disposed of. I suggested the dogs. Loyal animals defending him on his own property. I knew you were armed though. Thought you could handle it.'

'We shot and injured him.'

'You made a messy job of it. And it couldn't have happened to a nicer guy.'

'Who is he to you?'

'No friend.'

'Whose bodies are in the mill?'

There was a pause. 'So Connor's still welcoming guests there. I don't suppose business is any slower during the winter. And at least he doesn't have to worry about the heat ripening them up.'

'We had to call him a paramedic.'

'Did you?' he said, as if it was exactly the wrong thing to do. 'So where are you headed now?'

'You tell us.' She could hear his breath against the mouth-piece.

'Maybe you should be looking upriver. Connor's deliveries have to come from somewhere. Find cold storage. Security is going to be an issue for you though. I'll be waiting there with Abigail.'

'Wait. Let me speak to her.' But she knew he'd already hung up. 'What did he say?'

Holly composed herself and exhaled. 'That we should be looking upriver. Cold storage.' *What else could she do but obey?* She opened Google Maps on her phone and located the mill in the grounds of Waggity Camp. In the aerial photomap she could make out the snake of black water beside it. Fleet River, and it flowed into the estuary that fed into Peel Bay. She followed it inland and spotted a structure hugging one of the bends. 'That's got to be it.'

'What have you found?'

'Fresnade Meat Processing Plant.'

Maggie raised an eyebrow. 'So the family empire is bigger than we thought. How far?'

Holly tapped it into the satnav. 'Just over 4 miles.'

'We might not even make that.'

They both looked at the gas needle. They'd been running on empty for too long.

CHAPTER FIFTY-EIGHT

Three minutes later Maggie came across a gas station. It was set off from the trees on their right and stood alongside a log cabin diner. The neon under the green snow-covered canopy said it was open, but there was no sign of life in the booths or stools along the bar.

Maggie halted the car on the empty forecourt. 'Not a moment too soon.' She opened the door, swung her injured left leg out and blenched. It felt like the area around the bite re-ignited as soon as she put her weight on it.

'I'll fill it.' Holly put her hand on the door.

'No. It's fine.' She could see her jeans were tight around the swelling. 'Keep searching online.' Holly was trying to find out as much as she could about the Fresnades and their meat empire. If they were delivering bodies to the mill then they had to be prepared for their visit to the plant. Maggie levered herself out of the Scion and hobbled to the old school pump.

There was no attendant in the little wooden kiosk, so she started filling it herself. The sound of an engine turned her head back to the road. It was a patrol car, and it slowed beside the forecourt.

Maggie froze. The car had only just started filling up. *Should she pull the nozzle out of the tank, hang it up and get straight back in?* She glanced at Holly in the side mirror. She'd noticed it as well. Maggie nodded she'd seen it.

The patrol car pulled out of the blizzard, passed them and slid into the space beside the pump in front of the Scion. Maggie kept her finger on the trigger. If the policeman was here for gas it was better to do nothing that would draw attention to them.

The patrol car's engine was switched off and a female, uniformed officer got out. She was tall and slim, in her thirties, with a pale, freckled complexion and wore a hat with her red hair tucked up inside it. Her focus was on the kiosk, and she frowned at the empty window.

'Looks like Chet's gone AWOL again.' The police officer shook her head, but made her way over to the kiosk anyway.

Maggie smiled and rolled her eyes, as if she might know who Chet was.

The police officer peered in at the window and cupped her hand around her brow. 'Not crashed out in there either.'

Maggie hadn't seen her clock the licence plate when she got out of the patrol car but the rear one was quite visible now. And if the police were on the look-out for the two women who had fled Bozeman Street they probably had a description of them from Chuck Bretton. She darted her gaze to Holly as the officer strolled by the car. She was rigidly facing front.

The officer headed towards the diner, but swivelled back to Maggie. 'You'll have to pay in here. I'll see if I can find him.' She yanked the door and disappeared inside.

Maggie released the pump trigger. If they took off now without paying that would immediately arouse suspicion. *But was the officer already in there phoning their location in?*

Holly's window whirred down. 'What are we going to do?'

'I'll go in there. See what she's doing.'

'Shouldn't we just split?'

'She'll definitely alert other officers if we do that. I'll take a look. If she's not using her radio, I'll pay and come out as quickly as I can.' Maggie replaced the nozzle and shut the tank cover.

'Hurry then.'

Maggie limped to the door, straightened and girded herself to pace casually on her injury. She didn't want to start any conversations about it. Peering in through the pane she could see the police officer was standing at the counter with her back to Maggie, her head moving. She was talking to an older man with thinning white hair. *Was the officer just chatting to the cashier, or telling him there were two suspects on the forecourt?*

The man at the counter spotted Maggie. He said something and nodded at the door. The police officer turned, and her eyes fell on Maggie.

Maggie pretended she was on her way in and tugged the handle. As she entered she grinned and tried to discern if she'd interrupted the officer having a furtive discussion. 'Should I pay here?'

The police officer nodded but said nothing else.

Maggie reached the counter. 'The pump nearest the kiosk.'

The man behind the counter was wearing half spectacles. He tapped the register. 'That's um… $38.50.'

The police officer kept her body angled to the cashier and said nothing as Maggie fumbled out her charge card from her puffer jacket. She just had to keep cool until she paid and then they could hopefully leave without suspicion.

He indicated the reader beside the register.

She touched it with the card, and it beeped.

'Nasty.'

Maggie turned and found the officer examining her leg. 'Dog bite. Not as bad as it looks. My own fault. Shouldn't have taken on another stray.'

'Shouldn't you get that bandaged?'

'On my way to ER now. What a time to run out of gas.'

'Best be on your way then.' The cashier showed her his capped teeth.

Maggie felt the urge to hesitate. To make it clear to the officer she was prepared to answer any of her questions. 'Night.' She walked in silence, her bite throbbing tightly before she was at the door again. She pushed it and returned to the car.

Holly was sitting in the driver's seat and started up as soon as she appeared.

Maggie shook her head at her and got in. *Were they watching them on security cameras?*

'Well?'

'Still don't know.' Maggie swung the door shut. 'Wait a moment. Don't drive off too fast.'

They both waited while the engine puttered.

'OK. Don't look at the diner until we're at the ramp.'

Holly accelerated them slowly past it. As the car cut across to the exit side Maggie checked the officer in the side mirror. She was still standing at the counter, but had turned to watch them go.

'What d'you think?'

Maggie squinted. 'Don't pick up speed until we're out of earshot.'

Holly negotiated the car back into the storm and drove slowly up the road.

Maggie kept a watch on the diner until it had disappeared behind the trees. 'OK...' She consulted the satnav and found the nearest general. 'Thought so.'

'What's wrong?'

'Told them we were going to the hospital, and we've just left the wrong way.'

CHAPTER FIFTY-NINE

Hunched forward with her foot on the gas, Holly's position made her hip acutely uncomfortable.

'Want me to drive now?' Maggie offered.

'I'm fine. I'll take my turn.' Holly was glad to be at the wheel. The pain kept her awake and her mind away from speculating where Babysitter had taken Abigail.

After they'd covered a mile and there was still no sign of the patrol car in the mirror they both began to focus on the location ahead.

'So what do we know about the Fresnade family?'

'Take a look.' Holly passed her the phone. 'There's nothing online about them having any criminal associations.'

Maggie studied what Holly had found. 'Smart website.'

'They export a lot of canned meat to the military. The artisan smokery seems like their way of keeping the locals happy, but processed, mechanically recovered meat is their main source of income.'

'Mechanically recovered?'

Holly explained. 'Meat that's blasted off the bones of cattle after they've been slaughtered and the prime cuts have been taken. You won't find any images of that on the website.'

'How do you know about this?'

'I'm a vegetarian. Finding out what goes into those sorts of products was what made me become one.'

'So what do we think Babysitter's connection is?'

'Maybe he worked for them in the past. For the other side of the business.'

'The side that sends bodies downriver?'

Holly nodded. 'Why would they send bodies to the mill when they probably have the facilities to dispose of them at the plant though?'

'And what has any of this got to do with the East County Slayer?'

Holly knew the answer to that was still far from their grasp and daylight was fast approaching. 'Probably a good thing we didn't go calling on the Fresnades when we were in Brinkley.' She gritted her teeth against the stabbing in her hip. *Should she risk taking another pill?*

'They're not going to take too kindly to us turning up at their factory in the small hours. That's all he gave you to go on?'

'Just said that security was going to be an issue.'

'At a cannery in the middle of nowhere? Why would that be unless they've got something to hide? Let's hope there are no more dogs involved.' Maggie rubbed the exhaustion from her eyes.

A few moments later Holly turned right as the satnav instructed, and they headed down a tight, twisting road. 'This is taking us down to the river.'

The car channelled through deep, virgin snow.

'Doesn't look as if anyone has been down here since the storm began,' Maggie observed.

Holly studied the satnav. 'This isn't the only route in.'

'We'll get out a few minutes before we reach it. Go in on foot.'

Holly checked the dash again.

5:33 a.m.

Less than an hour and a half until sunrise.

'Babysitter could be trying to get someone else to dispose of us. Connor failed, maybe whoever we meet here won't.' Maggie's tone was grim.

'But Babysitter warned Connor.' Holly struggled to keep the Scion from skating right. 'Told him we were police. That's why he said we were spared.'

'That's what he told you. Maybe sending us here means he can be sure we'll never leave.'

They both fell silent as they wound closer to their destination.

CHAPTER SIXTY

Maggie kept her eye on the satnav. They were only a minute away from the plant, and she could feel apprehension slowly inflating. 'Pull over here.' She indicated a patch of dry ground under the overhang of a tree. The snow-laden branches were bowing, and as Holly positioned the Scion underneath them they were completely concealed from the road.

Holly peered to where the beam of the headlights penetrated the trees and then turned them off with the engine. The vista was suddenly black. She switched on her phone's flashlight. 'I think we should walk up to it through the forest.'

That made sense. Nobody would see them coming on the road and no obvious tracks. 'How much power have you got left?'

Holly checked the display. 'Eleven per cent.'

'Will that last us?' Maggie asked dubiously.

'Won't need it if we stay in the light at the edge of the trees.'

Maggie nodded. The snow on the road was faintly glowing from the smothered moon. They could follow it all the way there. 'OK, let's not waste any time.' She considered taking the shotgun from the back seat but didn't trust the thing. She still had bullets in her snubbie.

They both got out of the car and closed their doors. Holly led the way, her body bent as she limped under the lower branches. Maggie tried to keep the weight off her injured leg, but every slight tense of the muscle above her knee was agony.

'Wait.' Holly turned back in her direction.

Maggie stopped. 'What is it?' But under her breath she could hear a car approaching.

They both stepped back further into the foliage. The snow glowed yellow as a silver Hyundai appeared. It hissed by them and Maggie tried to glimpse who was sitting in the driver's seat.

It was a thickset man but through the falling flakes she could only see his silhouette as he passed.

They both waited for the engine to fade.

Holly was the first to speak. 'Lucky we got off the road. Did you see his face?'

'No. But he was pretty stocky. Don't think it was Babysitter.'

Holly hobbled along the rim of the road. 'We can't be far away.'

Maggie hoped Penny was fast asleep at Sascha's.

When they rounded the next bend they could see the taillights of the car. It was slowing down. Beyond it was a set of high wire gates.

'Come on!' Holly quickened her pace.

Maggie tried to keep up, but Holly had soon widened the gap. Ahead she could see a figure get out of the Hyundai and approach the gates. 'Slow down,' she hissed. 'He might hear you.'

Holly didn't until she was about twenty yards from the man. He was talking into an intercom on the cinder block wall beside the gates.

Maggie caught up with Holly, and they used the trees as cover, their bodies surging as they held their breaths inside.

The man turned from the wall, and they could clearly see his face. He was probably late forties and had a red trapper's hat on with flaps covering his ears. He jogged back to the car, and his flushed, double-chinned features clearly didn't relish it.

Maggie let out a breath and whispered. 'Definitely not Babysitter.'

Holly didn't reply, and they both watched him cram himself back in his seat, pull his door shut and wait.

'Let's get nearer.' Holly made to move forward.

'Careful. Don't let him see you in the rear-view.'

They stole further into the forest and covered the distance until they were adjacent to the Hyundai. The man impatiently puffed his cheeks.

The gates sluggishly opened. As soon as there was enough space between them he accelerated the car through. As he disappeared from sight the gates were still opening.

Holly turned to Maggie. 'What d'you think?'

Maggie could tell Holly was prepared to risk it.

'Might be the only chance we have to get inside.'

Maggie wondered if either of them could make it before the gates started closing again.

'Do we go?'

It seemed too good to be true. Maggie resisted the urge. 'No. And there's probably cameras.'

The gates finished opening and then paused a few seconds before closing.

Maggie pointed through the dense boughs to a visible section of the wall. 'Let's try and find another way in.'

Holly nodded, and they headed deeper into the forest.

CHAPTER SIXTY-ONE

Holly used her phone's flashlight to lead them to the snow-topped wall but it was at least ten feet high. 'You could boost me, and I'll take a look.' She licked a flake from her dry lips.

But Maggie was limping along the perimeter to the corner. 'Let's find out what's further along.'

'Why don't you wait here and rest? I'll go see.'

Maggie shook her head and continued: 'I'll let you know if I need a break.'

Holly caught up and lit the way. 'If they transport bodies downriver there must be an entrance near the bank.'

Maggie fell silent as they traversed the wall, and Holly got a whiff of something cooking: a heavy aroma of meat that had a sour edge. It became more overpowering the further they progressed.

A few minutes later they'd reached the end of it and hadn't encountered any other doors. Maggie halted at the corner.

They were at the top of a steep moonlit bank, and the river was flowing fast about fifty feet below. Holly switched off her flashlight and took in a large set of locked orange iron-panelled gates at the rear of the wall. In front of them was a wooden flight of steps to the water.

'No cameras.' Holly ventured out onto the bank and peered down the steps. There were a couple of powerboats moored up along a small boardwalk. She went to the gates. They were shorter than the wall. 'I can scale those.'

'Keep your head low.' Maggie interlaced her fingers and crouched.

Holly put her right foot on her palms and pushed up, hooking her hands over the top of the gate.

Maggie lifted her higher.

Holly could see over the edge of the gate and across a large snowbound loading bay. The back of the building had several shuttered doors. She scanned the walls for cameras, but couldn't spot any. 'Can you get me right over?' Holly felt Maggie's wrists trembling as she grunted and thrust her foot again.

Her wound burnt but Holly bent her left leg over the edge of the gate and shifted her body so she was lying along it.

'If you drop down, you won't be able to get back up.'

But Holly could see the gates were only locked with a giant bolt. 'Doesn't matter.' She swung herself over and thudded onto the thick snow. She sucked in breath to stem the pain, shot the iron bolt as quietly as she could and opened one of the gates inwards.

Maggie hobbled through, and Holly shut it again, leaving the bolt out in case they needed to leave in a hurry.

'No sign of dogs yet.' Holly swept her eyes warily around the loading bay. 'Or our friend in his car.' She started crossing the snow.

'Somebody let him in too.' Maggie followed unsteadily.

Holly glanced back at their footprints. Hopefully they'd be filled in before the morning.

The shutters were padlocked to metal hoops embedded in the yard.

'D'you think this is where cold storage is?' Holly craned up to the dark windows, but they were about thirty feet above them.

They trod quietly along the wall and came to a fire exit. That was sealed too.

Holly and Maggie passed giant air vents above their heads belching out the sour steam. They reached the corner of the building. Fifty yards away was another smaller, modern, two-storey facility. The silver Hyundai was parked in front of it, and there were lights burning on both floors.

Holly craned around the first building. Ten feet along was a flight of stone steps leading up to a navy blue door. 'Shall we find out if it's open?'

Maggie was still focussed on the windows of the smaller building. 'Wait.'

The stocky guy emerged from its glass door and they both ducked back.

They waited as his heavy footsteps creaked across the snow towards them.

Maggie jerked her thumb behind them. But even if they quickly scrambled back the way they'd just come he'd still catch sight of them.

The crunching got louder, and Holly's hand rested on the gun in her poncho.

CHAPTER SIXTY-TWO

Maggie clenched her teeth and felt her circulation thud in her throat. He'd almost reached them. Maggie pointed at Holly's breath that was escaping in clouds. She sealed her mouth. The footfalls halted then sped up and changed in pitch.

He was climbing the steps to the door. They heard the handle and then it swing open and shut. Maggie exchanged a look with Holly.

There was no need for discussion. Keeping her attention on the smaller building, Maggie hesitantly followed his deep footprints up the steps towards the navy blue entrance. No movement in the windows opposite. Holly was close behind. Maggie put her palm on the cold metal of the handle and pulled it down. As she cracked the door, a draught of warm air and the concentrated smell of cooked meat gushed out.

Beyond was a changing room. A row of plastic white overalls were hanging on hooks. There was no sign of the man who had just entered. Maggie hastened inside. The sooner they were off the front steps the better. Holly carefully clicked the door shut behind them.

Maggie nodded to the next blue door that led out of the changing room and crossed the grey tiled floor to it. Holly tapped her on the shoulder and pointed at the overalls. Maggie nodded again, and they took one each off a hook and briskly slid them on.

The overall was thin and smelt strongly of plastic. As they paused by the door to listen for any sounds, Maggie noticed a box of white elasticated hats that looked like shower caps. She handed one to

Holly, and they both donned them before Maggie depressed the handle and peered outside.

They edged into a long corridor with more blue doors along it. Some open, others closed. They passed the first and could see it was a communal area. There was a coffee machine, microwave and lots of dirty paper cups scattered over a low table surrounded by plastic chairs.

Where had the stocky guy disappeared? There were another six doors either side of the corridor. Maggie tried the first and was looking into a unisex bathroom.

A slam from the end of the corridor. They waited, motionless but nobody emerged from any of the doors so they made their way cautiously to the last one. Maggie tugged it.

She was looking down a short corridor to a large set of blue double doors. Another warm gust and they could hear machinery rumbling. Pushing through them they were confronted by an expansive high-ceilinged room, silver pipes ran across its girders and there was a tall bank of chrome industrial food processors before them. No sign of the stocky guy or anyone else.

'Let's try and find cold storage.' Maggie led the way through two large grinders. If they ran into anyone it was unlikely the overalls would sell their presence there. There were no other workers around. They covered the polished white floor, passing several huge silver canisters that vibrated deep in her chest.

There was a sign hanging over the next piece of apparatus. Maybe it could point them in the right direction.

But as she squinted at it a figure turned into their walkway. It was the stocky guy, minus his hat and coat.

He stopped dead. 'Who the fuck are you two?' His few strands of dark hair were plastered to his scalp.

'Night shift,' Holly answered immediately.

'Bullshit. How did you get in?' His beady eyes darted, and he loped forward again.

Maggie immediately pulled her gun.

'Jesus.' He froze and raised his hands as high as his chin. 'If you're cops you'd better have a warrant.'

'Anything you want to tell us?' Maggie wondered if he had any colleagues nearby.

'Let me see the warrant first.' He put out his hand.

Maggie noticed it was shaking. 'You seem very nervous.'

'You're pointing a gun at me.' But he was examining the weapon in her hand and frowning. 'You ain't cops.'

Holly pulled out hers.

'Easy,' Maggie cautioned her.

'What is this?'

Maggie clocked a security camera in the ceiling above him. 'The only relevant fact is that we're holding the guns. Just take us to cold storage.'

'What?' But a brief spark of panic registered in his gaze.

'You heard me.' Maggie took a pace towards him.

'There's no cold storage.'

'We don't have time for this,' Maggie snapped. 'You've got three seconds to do it or we'll find somebody else.'

'I'm the only one here.'

'Liar.' Maggie knew somebody had let him in. 'Do it now.'

But Holly was suddenly choking beside her before an arm locked around Maggie's neck. She struggled but, as the solid bicep cut off her oxygen, her vision went gradually yellow then quickly black.

CHAPTER SIXTY-THREE

Maggie slapped Holly's face. 'Come on. We haven't been out too long.'

Holly sat up, coughed and clutched her throat.

Maggie's was tender too. 'Our guns have been taken.' They'd also had their overalls removed. Maggie helped her stand.

Holly briefly tottered as she took in the tiny room, which was bare. Just a concrete floor, strip lights and another blue door.

'I've tried it. Locked.' Maggie still felt shaky on her feet as well.

Holly went to it regardless and wrenched the handle. 'Let us out!' she yelled.

'They're probably deciding what to do with us.' Maggie surveyed the room again. There was an air vent in the grey plaster wall opposite them, but the grill was tiny.

Holly kicked the panel beside the handle with the sole of her right boot. It was solid, and she gasped as her leg absorbed the impact.

'Just take a breath.'

'No time to.' Holly clenched herself in readiness for a second attempt but there was a noise outside.

Footfalls.

They both remained rigid as they drew nearer. Sounded like at least two people.

'If you could just step back from the door.' The male voice was clear and conciliatory.

Didn't sound to Maggie like the stocky guy.

'I'm with some associates but I'd like the opportunity to speak to you alone. If you can promise me you'll behave I'll persuade them to stay outside. Agreed?'

Neither of them replied.

'Agreed?'

'Yes,' Holly responded.

The lock snapped, and the door opened gently inwards. A face came around the edge much lower than Maggie expected.

The slim and diminutive man checked their position and then slid inside and closed the door with his back. He was wearing a faded red sweatshirt with 'Dark Revolution Craft Beer' written on it, black denims and brown leather loafers. He looked to be in his fifties but had a healthy head of shoulder-length dark brown hair with only a few flecks of grey in it. 'I'm Howie,' he said, like he was about to commence a tour.

Maggie knew they shouldn't be fooled by his casual appearance and demeanour. 'What are we doing in here, Howie?'

'That was going to be my question. You're trespassing on my private property.'

'Then why haven't you called the cops?'

His grey eyes slid to Holly. 'Thought I'd find out first what you expected to score at a meat cannery. Apart from the obvious.'

Was he a Fresnade? 'We're not here to rob you. But you know that.' Maggie studied his reaction.

He shrugged good-naturedly. 'So if you're not here for that, what then?'

'Cold storage.'

He frowned at Maggie, a little too hard. 'My associate said you'd mentioned that.'

'Let's just cut to the chase with this.' Maggie held his gaze to sell the bluff.

He shook his head. 'Sorry. I feel dumb. You'll have to elaborate.'

'It's over.' Holly assisted the deceit.

'Over? Now that is a crying shame. But if only I knew what you were talking about.'

But Maggie could see the unease in his scrutiny. 'We've got people waiting for us outside these walls. If we don't come back, the cops will be here in minutes.'

'Not in this weather. And you still haven't told me why you've broken in and exactly what it is you want.' The civility had drained from his expression.

'Money.' Maggie was sure he was hiding something.

'Money?' He nodded and pursed his lips for effect. 'Got a figure in mind?'

'Fifty thousand.'

His eyes flickered amusement. 'And what is it that my money will actually buy me?'

'Silence.' Maggie could see something else lurking in his regard, malice skulking behind his act. Suddenly she got the impression they were sharing a room with an individual neither of them was remotely capable of handling.

CHAPTER SIXTY-FOUR

Holly didn't doubt that, if she rushed Howie, Maggie would help her overpower him. *But what would happen when they got to the other side of the door? It could be their only chance of escape though…*

'So you want to blackmail me?' he scoffed.

Maggie briefly shrugged her shoulders. 'Call it what you want.'

'So you'll stay silent about what if I give you this fifty grand?'

'Nobody has to know about cold storage.'

Holly knew Maggie was about to run out of leverage. 'And you'd better let us out of here right now. Our friends have explicit instructions.'

'I'm sure they have. But as I've got nothing to hide why don't you call them?' He pulled Holly's phone from his pocket and held it out to her.

'I will… after you step aside and we've walked.' But Holly saw her brief hesitation had told Howie everything he needed to know.

He withdrew his arm. 'You're acting alone.'

'She's told you; we'll only call them when we're free.' Maggie remained defiant. 'If we don't make it out they're going to be sending the cops right to your door.'

'How long?'

'How long what?' But Holly understood exactly what he was asking her.

'How long before these friends of yours bring in the cavalry?'

Holly looked at her watch.

6:32 a.m.

Less than half an hour until sunrise. *What did that mean for Abigail?*

'A couple of hours,' Maggie answered for her.

'That's quite a window. If you were afraid something might happen to you wouldn't you want them to come sooner? Or are you giving your story plenty of time?'

'Pass me my phone.' Holly extended her hand.

Howie shook his head once and pocketed it. 'I think we've established there's nobody waiting out there. And I'm not about to give you the phone so you can call anyone else.'

'See what happens then. If they don't—'

'Shut the fuck up,' he cut Maggie off sharply. 'You've wasted enough of my time. I'll let you both go but you have to tell me exactly who you are and who put you up to this.'

'Look… we're cops.' Maggie tried to make it sound like a reluctant confession.

'Don't bother with that. Tell me the truth. Lester!'

The door opened. Holly expected somebody big to walk through it, but the man who appeared was lean and only slightly taller than Howie. He wore a grubby black and white varsity jacket and loose jeans. A dyed dark goatee hugged his gaunt features, and the peak of his jagged denim baseball cap was pulled low so his sunken sockets were in shadow.

'I heard.' Lester stepped past Howie.

Holly saw he had the fingers of his left hand through the holes of a brass knuckleduster and that his right held a hypodermic needle.

'You don't want to fuck with Lester.' Howie turned, took a key from his jeans pocket and locked the door.

Holly swallowed and couldn't disguise it.

'You don't scare us,' Maggie said scornfully.

Howie closed his eyes. 'Who put you up to this?'

Lester took a few paces towards Holly.

'Don't.'

'Touch her and you'll have me to deal with,' Maggie threatened.

But Holly was sure Howie would rush Maggie while Lester was taking care of her.

'Just make this easy on yourselves. You're gonna tell me everything I want to know but it's up to you if you want to get brain damage in the process.'

'Stay back!' Holly yelled as Lester playfully jinked sideways and then forwards towards her.

'Now I'm sure there's nobody waiting for you, we've got plenty of time.' Howie remained by the door. 'Fifty grand? You're both gonna make me so much more than that. While we're doing what we're about to do to you and you're begging us to stop, one second, one fucking second of that will make me fifty grand.'

Holly figured they were in the middle of a bigger situation than either of them had envisaged. 'Just let us walk out of here.' She couldn't keep the fear out of her voice. 'Stay back!'

Lester advanced.

'Just wait!' Maggie raised her palms. 'We don't know anything. That's the truth. We were sent in here. All we were told were those two words "cold storage".'

Howie puffed his cheeks in mock relief. 'So you're *not* threatening to blackmail me now?'

'She's telling the truth.' But Holly knew the bluff had badly backfired. 'Somebody has my child. I need to find her.'

Lester momentarily froze.

Howie lifted an eyebrow. 'Your child?'

She nodded. 'We were told to come here. We've no idea why. We don't know what cold storage is.'

His features were impassive. 'Hear that, Lester?'

He nodded the peak of his baseball cap.

'Think we should help these ladies out?'

Lester grinned so his goatee stretched tight.

Holly barrelled at Lester. She could knock the hypodermic from his grip. Maggie headed towards Howie.

Holly swung for Lester's face.

Lester's pockmarked expression was unperturbed by her assault. Stepping effortlessly sideways he lifted the needle high and swiped once at Holly with the knuckleduster.

CHAPTER SIXTY-FIVE

Maggie shivered and could smell bleach. The aroma stung her nostrils, and she cracked her eyes as other sensations of pain crowded in. The worst was in her arms. The light in the room was dazzling but, as she recoiled, it dimmed. She felt drunk and, as she stiffened, could feel the ache in both shoulder sockets intensify.

The dirty white tiled floor spun. She was hanging and gazed up at her wrists secured by rope and threaded through a metal loop in the ceiling. The light got bright again as she swung back around, and tried to squint at who was standing beside it.

'Welcome to cold storage,' Howie stated flatly.

Maggie's legs felt numb as she tried to move them. She peered down to where the soles of her boots were against the floor and attempted to stand. She wobbled on them and tipped sideways. 'What did you give me?' she snarled into a glowing bulb and saw it was on a black stand and had four metallic flaps about it like a movie light.

'Just a sedative to make you sleep while we set things up. But we want you wide awake to experience everything now.'

'Untie me.' She weakly stood erect and relieved the tension in her arms.

'Who told you about this place?'

Maggie dizzily stumbled sideways and yelled as her arms took all her weight again. Beyond Howie, Maggie could see Holly. She was restrained like her, her head bowed, with the stocky guy standing in front of her. He wasn't touching Holly just looking her over, as if sizing her up. *Where was Lester?*

Howie's engrossed expression came into focus. He was study-ing the viewer of a camera that was positioned on a tripod. 'We'll livestream after we've had a little chat. Then we'll be giving you injections to keep you awake.'

Behind Howie was a low table with a laptop on it. Next to him was a tubular metal surgeon's trolley. There were implements arranged along it, but Maggie couldn't make out what they were before her body pivoted away.

'Lester has gone to slip into something more comfortable. He bagged you. Think it's that wound on your left knee. Bet he's got a whole shit bunch of ideas about that. Lester can be very creative.'

Maggie gripped the rope and heaved herself upright.

'Tell me how you came to know about this place.' Howie sounded distracted.

Maggie turned on her heels. He was still entranced by the viewer. Now she could see what was on the trolley. Only a few of the implements were surgical. Next to the scalpels there was a nail gun, a mini blowtorch, a selection of hypodermics, some clear plastic bottles of liquid and a wire brush.

'Just speak into the lens.' Howie's attention didn't shift from the mini screen at the back of the camera.

'We told you. Somebody has her child. They told us to come here. After we'd been to the kennels.' She had to give him more.

Howie briefly met the gaze of the stocky guy.

Lying hadn't worked. *Could she delay whatever had been planned for them by telling him about Babysitter and the journey he'd sent them on?* He was clearly a threat to Howie's vile operation.

'And?'

'We met Connor.' She wouldn't say he was now in the hands of the police.

Howie sucked his bottom lip. 'What happened?'

'Untie us both. I'll tell you everything.'

'You don't get to make any demands… Sorry…' He shrugged his shoulders. 'I don't know your name.'

'Let me down and I'll tell you.'

'But I need to call you something. You look like a Jenny. Never met a bad Jenny. I'll call you that.' He slightly lowered the camera on the tripod.

She felt panic rise. He seemed fixed on whatever he was going to do. 'We saw the mill. We went inside.' Maggie registered Holly slightly raise her head but the stocky guy was too busy concentrating on their conversation. She had to keep both men distracted. Howie would want to find out exactly how much more she knew.

His jaw muscle twitched. 'If you've been to the mill then you're familiar with exactly where you're going to end up. Connor's movies are a little more esoteric, but he services a significant demand. I prefer to deal with the living. What he does with you afterwards is between him and the clients who pay to watch him in action.'

Maggie felt repulsed but could tell Howie was still thinking about what she'd said. 'I'll give up the guy who told us. But you get us down. Now.'

Howie mock considered it. 'Hmm… or, I could start with your friend over there. Take her clothes off and then peel her skin strip by strip. It's a long process but we've got all sorts of time.'

Maggie watched the stocky guy turn back to Holly.

'Hey, she's back with us.' He lifted her head by grabbing her hair and yanking it up.

'Perfect timing.' Howie met Maggie's eye. 'So what's it to be? Watch her being done before you so you can see what's going to happen, or fess up and die first?'

Maggie knew it wasn't a threat to make her talk. He was going to kill them both.

The stocky guy plodded over to the laptop.

'Lester, for fuck's sake hurry it up!' Howie yelled.

There was movement at the rear of the room.

At first Maggie thought Lester was naked. But as his figure entered the periphery of the light she could see he was wearing a transparent catsuit. It looked like it was made of thin yellow rubber. A zipped pocket at the front accommodated his genitalia. He kicked off his black flip flops and twisted the object in his hand. He fumbled the pea green mask onto his shaved head. Only his eyes were visible through the slits, but small white dots delineated his concealed features.

'Something new we're fucking with. Haden here,' Howie nodded at the stocky guy, 'he can put one of our client's faces where Lester's is. So it looks like whatever Lester's doing to you, they're doing to you.'

The fact they were using their names so freely meant they never expected her to repeat them. Maggie's eyes flitted from Lester to Howie to Haden.

'And as I've just let my clients know we've got two in cold storage they're all eager to do some truly fucked-up shit.'

CHAPTER SIXTY-SIX

Holly had been listening to the conversation for a few minutes when Haden had dragged her head up and a glimpse at her bonds above confirmed it was going to be impossible to free herself.

Although her temple throbbed from whatever blow she'd sustained, she could feel the strength gradually returning to her limbs. But Holly could barely support herself on her feet. Keeping her face to the floor she took in the room through her curtain of curls.

'Plenty of requests here.' Haden squinted at the laptop screen.

Howie leaned close to Maggie. 'Where do we start with your friend? Or are you going to make this easier on yourself?'

Maggie refused to meet his eye. 'He calls himself Babysitter.'

Holly knew Maggie was running out of information to give him. But the mention of the name had silenced Howie.

Holly noticed Lester turn in his direction.

'Babysitter?' Howie shot a look at Lester. 'And what do you know about *him*?'

'Only seen him twice.' Maggie reeled but righted herself. 'But we're meant to be meeting him this morning.'

Holly knew what Maggie was doing. If they could convince their captors they could lead them to Babysitter, maybe they'd be momentarily spared.

'She told us they had people waiting outside.' Lester's mask muffled his voice. 'And that was bullshit.' He was eager to continue.

'We couldn't tell you about Babysitter. He's kidnapped her child.' Maggie turned to Holly.

Holly dipped her head again. Better they thought she was still semi-conscious.

'It couldn't be Pauly,' Lester said sceptically to the others.

'Why not?' Howie challenged.

'Your brother took care of him. Said he dumped him in the Fleet.'

'My brother said a lot of things.' Howie sounded deep in thought. 'You say you met him a couple of times. How old was this guy? What did he look like?'

'Mid-twenties maybe. Square jaw, thick eyebrows, slit-up nose.'

Holly waited for the three men to absorb the description and prayed it was the right one.

Howie spoke first. 'That's our Pauly.'

'Fucking Pauly?' Lester scoffed.

Holly raised her head so she could see again.

'Where are you meeting him?' Howie gripped the rope securing Maggie's wrists.

Maggie was silent.

'I've told you what we can do to your friend.'

'He won't show unless we do. He's been following us. If we don't walk out of here he'll probably vanish.'

'Nice try,' Haden scoffed.

Howie held up a hand. 'So he took your friend's baby. Why?'

'He took mine first. Said he'd only return her to me if I killed a woman named Janet Braun.'

Howie folded his arms. 'And did you?'

Maggie slowly nodded.

CHAPTER SIXTY-SEVEN

Holly forgot the pain of her restraints as Maggie's admission briefly halted the interrogation. *Was she attempting to dupe them?* But Holly had suspected Maggie might have been lying to her since the first time they'd spoken through the bedroom door.

'I stabbed Janet.'

Holly was riveted to Maggie's deadpan features.

'She was told to do the same.' Maggie indicated Holly, but the men didn't turn. 'Broke into my home and tried to kill me. Who's Pauly?'

Howie briefly grimaced. 'Not your concern. All you have to do is tell us where you're supposed to be meeting him.'

'I told you, if we're not there, he's not going to show.'

Holly held her breath.

Lester tugged off the mask. He seemed agitated. 'She's full of it.'

'It's a fucked-up story. Which is why I believe it.' Howie stared unblinkingly at Maggie. 'What's the purpose of the meeting?'

'I don't know. We're just following his instructions.'

'Doesn't make sense. If he sent you in here to find cold storage, the chances were you wouldn't be leaving again. Maybe this meeting is bullshit. His or yours.'

'It's not,' Holly interrupted. Four heads swivelled to her but she needed to shift the focus from Maggie before things got too intense. 'But neither of us is going to tell you where we agreed to meet because that's the only thing keeping us alive.'

'That's cute. But you will tell us.' Howie uncrossed his arms. 'Really, it'll take minutes. I take it you have a time for this meeting?'

'Yes.' Holly barely cracked the word.

Howie suddenly crossed the room to her and bent his ear to her lips. 'Just whisper to me what it is then.'

His head was completely blocking Maggie.

'Nine this morning, OK?' Maggie blurted out.

Howie stood, jaw muscle twitching.

It had been a test. Holly would have whispered. Then he would have got Maggie to do the same. If the times hadn't tallied he would have known they were lying. Maggie had removed the threat.

'In a wharf parking lot,' Maggie added before he could silence her. 'Near some net lofts.'

Holly knew exactly to where she was referring. Even if they were separately interrogated now they both had the same location in mind.

'But neither of us will tell you more than that until we're in a car driving there.'

'Bravo.' Howie pulled his sleeve back to glimpse his watch and strolled back to Maggie. 'But if this meeting's not until nine I can find out what your names are, even who the first guy who fucked you was. I know already who'll be the last.' He briefly rested his hand on Lester's shoulder.

'He won't show himself if we're not there.' Holly managed to stand straight.

'So you both keep saying,' Howie murmured thoughtfully.

'Are we going to waste our time with this crap any longer?' Lester gestured to the laptop. 'We can't keep the clients waiting.'

'If we've been compromised, I'm not comfortable continuing.' Haden put his hands in his pockets.

Lester huffed. 'Jesus, you're such a chicken shit. Are we really afraid of Pauly?'

Haden's beady eyes darted to Howie. 'Tie them up and drive them out to this rendezvous. If it's bullshit, we slit their throats.'

Holly was positive the matter-of-fact way he said it meant it certainly wasn't a ploy to scare them.

Howie considered it.

'Really?' Lester was impatient. 'They're just playing for time.'

And that's all they had. When they got back to Astley, Holly was sure it would be over. But at least that way they'd maybe have an opportunity to escape.

Howie sucked his teeth. 'Tell me now if I'm wasting my time, girls.'

Neither of them spoke.

'Because if he's a no-show then we bring you both back here. I'll keep you alive for days. If you don't want that, one of you speak the truth now.'

'It IS the truth,' Holly said before Maggie could.

Howie studied Maggie, and she slowly blinked.

'Fuck this.' Lester removed his surgical gloves and slapped them onto the trolley. 'What if we get caught?'

'Nobody's out in this weather,' Howie placated.

'But we might get stuck in a drift. It was difficult enough getting over here tonight.'

'He's got a point.' Haden flattened a strand of hair to his flushed pate.

'Both you boys are coming. We can't sedate them if we want them to get out of the truck when we get there, so I'll need you two to strong-arm them.'

Haden shuffled on the balls of his feet. 'I didn't sign up for this. I'm your tech man.'

'You've never objected to pacifying the girls and boys before.' Howie raised an eyebrow. 'Not in your remit either but you always get a shot when Lester's done.'

Haden looked suddenly self-conscious.

'Where else would you be allowed to do what you do down here? Huh?'

Haden's expression softened.

'Come on.' Howie clicked his fingers twice. 'I need your help.'

Haden returned his attention to Holly. 'I get to finish *her*, agreed?'

Howie nodded, benevolently. 'Sure. After we've cut the feed you can take as long as you like with her.'

Haden smiled coyly at Holly, like she'd consented, and a cold wave of dread broke over her.

'So I got to get changed now?' Lester pointed at the laptop. 'What about them?'

Howie picked up the wire brush from the trolley. 'They'll have to wait. We can't pass this up.'

'Fuck's sake. Give me a couple of minutes.' Lester slipped his feet back into his flipflops.

Howie pressed the metal bristles hard against Maggie's left cheek. 'We're going to take you down now but every time you disobey I take off a layer of your face with this. Clear?'

Maggie didn't make a sound but nodded.

Howie jabbed his finger at Holly. 'Same goes for you.'

Holly felt hatred for him reviving her.

Howie removed the brush and reached up to the hook above Maggie's head. 'Haden, can you let our clients know we're experiencing technical difficulties. Something to do with the weather maybe.'

He didn't reply.

But Holly could see why he hadn't. The yellow twin wires of a taser were sticking out of his back, and his body had gone into spasm.

CHAPTER SIXTY-EIGHT

Maggie watched Haden's expression distort as his whole frame jerked and thought he might be having an attack. But as soon as he dropped to his knees and rolled onto his side she could see the owner of the taser that his body had been blocking.

It was the man who had threatened her in the car. The man who had taken Penny from the lot. Babysitter. Pauly. And he had a red fire axe in his other hand.

Howie turned as Babysitter dumped the gun connected to the wires, and it clunked to the tiles. 'Pauly, what the fuck is this?'

Babysitter didn't hesitate and swung the axe at Howie.

'Don't, don't!' Howie held out his hands to bootlessly protect himself, but the blade lodged into his chin and sternum, pinning his head firmly to his chest, the thud and crunch sickening.

Maggie reversed away from them as Howie remained motionless. She was totally exposed.

Babysitter put his boot against Howie's chest and yanked the blade free. Howie teetered, but remained standing, suspended in shock.

Lester had retreated to where Holly was hanging. 'It's me, Pauly. Remember? Lester.'

Babysitter strode over to him, knuckles white on the handle. 'Fuck!'

Babysitter raised the axe and swiped it at the side of Lester's terrified face. It pulverised his left cheekbone but then bounced away. Lester fell against the wall screaming.

Babysitter brought the axe down, and this time it lodged deep in Lester's left shoulder. Blood gushed out of the wound and started filling up his latex catsuit.

Babysitter put his boot against his gashed features and waggled out the axe.

Maggie registered Howie clutching himself and heading into the darkness beyond the movie light, a trail of blood behind him.

Babysitter slammed the axe into his spine, and it flattened him to the floor. Howie lay sprawled on his front, whimpering, and Babysitter stood on the back of his head and hauled the blade from him. He arced it repeatedly at his prostrate form, the impacts on bone making the soles of his loafers bounce off the tiles.

Maggie counted eleven blows long after he'd started.

Babysitter's attention returned to Lester. He was sobbing and now looked like he was wearing a dark red suit.

Maggie closed her eyes as he silenced him with equal ferocity. The sound of metal striking his limbs made her cringe with every blow.

'Maggie,' a breathless voice whispered at her ear.

She kept her lids closed and felt the draught of his hot, sour, irregular panting against them.

He gulped and sniffed. 'Open up.'

She complied and saw he was standing beside her, his face only an inch from her.

He leaned forward on the handle of the axe and allowed the blade to take his weight. His dark bomber jacket glistened, and there was a fine spray of blood over his square features and split nose. The backs of his hands were red and sticky, and his exertions had clearly drained him. 'Been a while since I've been down here.' He swallowed. 'Lester hasn't changed. Think he dyes his beard now though.'

Maggie twisted her head to look at where Lester lay against the wall. The axe had mashed his face and shoulders, his catsuit had been shredded and his blood was rapidly pooling around him.

Maggie met Holly's stunned expression. They were both helpless.

'Don't know this guy.' Babysitter turned to where Haden was still curled on the floor. 'But anybody working for Howie…' He hefted the axe again and chopped into Haden.

'Stop!' Holly yelled.

Babysitter looked down at Haden and drew in a faltering breath.

Maggie couldn't retreat any further, and there was no way she could free herself from the metal loop above her. 'We've done everything you asked of us.'

Babysitter nodded. 'You didn't find me though. I found you.'

'You're Pauly. You worked with these…' Maggie couldn't find the words.

'I worked *for* them. Major difference. I was in front of the camera. But then I became a babysitter.'

Maggie took in Howie's splayed corpse behind him.

'Fifteen years old and happy to let anyone else have their turn in front of the cameras instead of me.'

'These people.' Holly tried to keep her voice steady. 'They're vermin. Whatever they were doing here had to be stopped.'

Maggie knew Holly was trying to sympathise with him, but suspected it was futile.

'I brought kids here. Duped them. To protect myself.' He looked around him. 'I trapped them, like Tom Fresnade trapped me. He was a councillor at camp. When the orphans' bus rolled in it must have been like Christmas to him and Howie. That's when they got me. They knew how to select. I wanted older friends who would stand up for me. I didn't want to be the helpless kid. Would have done anything to be them. They gave me beer and cigarettes and made me part of their scene. They took me to the smokery to party. That's where they started all this – before their old man died. Lester spiked my drink. Showed me the recording the next day.' Babysitter put the axe on the trolley, and it made the implements on it bounce and rattle. 'I brought in the other kids. And after I watched them go through the same ordeal, I gave them Pepsis and told them it had all happened to me and that I was still fine. And when they cried like I had I didn't have any sympathy for them because they reminded me of who I'd been.'

Maggie watched the vein pump at the side of his neck as he examined the tools on the trolley.

'But Tom Fresnade was my saviour. He drove me out to High-cliff one night. Told me I was getting too old. Howie wanted me gone. *Dead* gone. Even though I could never talk – after all, I had helped transport enough bodies down to the mill to Connor. I'd dropped out of high school. Nobody would have missed me, but Tom let me go. Said he'd tell Howie he'd done the job. He gave me money and told me to get on the bus. When I left him he was more scared than me. He saved my life that night. I don't think Howie ever allowed him to stop. I like to think he gladly gave himself to the water after diving in to save Rich Temple's kids. Chances are though, if he hadn't he'd be lying here now.' He gazed down at Haden's body. 'Howie's diversified in the time I've been gone. His client base is worldwide now. Not just a sleazy cabal of local businessmen.'

'Please,' Holly implored. 'Tell me where Abigail is.'

'Abigail will be spared. She was always a means to an end.'

The two women locked eyes. *Another trick?*

CHAPTER SIXTY-NINE

'After I escaped I started looking for my birth parents. It became an obsession. Who would I have been if they hadn't thrown me away? Family was what I always craved – that was what had drawn me to Tom Fresnade. I never traced my father. Not even a vague lead to him. I found my mother though. She'd been unmarried and had me in St Thomas's, a hospital for the homeless. It's been pulled down now. She'd died giving birth to me. Not during the rigours of childbirth. A woman in similar circumstances walked into her room and stabbed her with a carving knife. She'd lost her baby years before and had been driven mad by the grief. It was a random attack. My mother, Edina Young, tried to fight her off. Maternal instincts can be so powerful. But she died. Liz Sangster, the woman who murdered her, hung herself in her prison cell less than a year later. I survived…' He trailed off, then touched his split nose thoughtfully. 'A blessing for me. Or for these people anyway.' Babysitter glanced around at the mutilated bodies. 'But I'm building a new family now. The babies that are taken into care when they lose their mothers in the same way I did, when they're old enough, I'll reach out to them and tell them how our butchered childhoods connect us.'

Holly's body locked tight. Whatever warped sense his plan made to him the purpose was clear: he wanted Abigail for himself. And she wasn't ever going to allow that.

'Let us go, Pauly.' Maggie's voice was level. 'If anything happens to Holly or me there's a recording going straight to the police…'

'We'll come to that when we're done here. But it's likely you won't be part of that conversation, Maggie. Not if you're the committed mother I think you are.' He picked up the scalpel from the tray. 'It's fortunate we have the privacy of this place. It used to be the underground icehouse, when this was a groceries depository in the thirties. Fresnade senior thought Howie had it bricked up. Don't know how many drifters and vagrants ended up down here, but with those and the casual student labour the packing plant relied on, Howie always had a fresh supply of subjects for his movies. Now, which one of you wants to have their ropes cut?' He turned to Holly.

Holly regarded the blade in his hand and immediately knew what he intended.

'I can only release one of you. But I'm happy for you to have a discussion between yourselves and decide who it'll be. Although I think we all already know.' He took a step back, as if it would afford them more space to talk.

Maggie lurched and readjusted her footing. 'Cut us both down. We've told you we'll guarantee our silence.'

'If I let Abigail and Penny live?'

'Yes.'

'I found your sister's place, Maggie. Know how much she likes to look after Penny. I could be there in no time.'

'You son of a bitch. I did what you asked of me,' Maggie spat.

'And I returned Penny.'

Holly closed her eyes. Even though she wanted to believe Maggie had been lying to Howie she couldn't now.

'And if neither of us wants to be freed?' Maggie asked before Holly could.

'Then…' he sighed. 'You'll have to forfeit both your children, and I'll find two more women who will make better mothers than you. I can lock you in here and leave you to rot with these three.'

'Just untie us, Pauly. Let us help you.' Holly softened her tone. 'We know you've suffered…' her voice faltered. 'You have the power to end this.'

Babysitter ignored her. 'Your time is short, Maggie. I know about your visits to the oncologist. You must see that your sacrifice is the answer to this situation. If I let Holly go and she kills you, Penny only loses a mother for months less than she would have anyway.'

Maggie's expression radiated hatred.

'And you could even give Holly here your blessing to look after Penny. Can't you see how this could work out for your daughter? And isn't she all that's important?'

Holly knew they had to keep him talking and stall the moment he'd designed for them. 'So your chain remains unbroken, and the cops keep looking for the East County Slayer.'

Babysitter opened his arms. 'That elusive male figure, isn't he significant to all of us?'

'And someone for you to hide behind while you ruin the lives of innocent children,' Maggie said with disdain. 'And when do you kill Holly?'

'Why would I need to do that? If she turns herself in to the police after murdering you she may never see her child again, never make good on her promise to care for Penny and make your death meaningful, Maggie.'

Holly's fists clenched tight in her bonds. 'Liar. You're not going to stop. If you were, you would have after the first child you orphaned. You'll get somebody else to silence me.'

He swivelled slowly to her. 'You are at least considering it then?'

'We'll both be silent. We promise. Right, Maggie?'

Maggie nodded.

'Too complicated.'

'But, like you say, it won't be for long.' Maggie tried to meet his eye.

But his attention was on Holly. 'You should have killed Maggie in the house. You'd have Abigail back by now. But now you have to take the life of your new friend. You'll be guaranteeing her child a stable future as well as yours though. Use that. Maggie did it for her child. You'll only be doing what any mother would.'

Would she be dead soon after Maggie? But what would he do with Abigail? Did he really expect her to be mother to her and Penny until whatever time he decided to become part of the children's lives? Or would he seal both their bodies in the icehouse with those of his tormentors and take the children whenever he wanted?

'OK. We've debated this enough. You've got ten seconds and then I'm closing this place up. You'll have nothing to do down here but wonder what's happened to your children while you slowly starve to death. Holly, Abigail's back home but she'll need feeding soon. Are you both going to make the right decision?'

CHAPTER SEVENTY

Holly swung her eyes to Maggie but she was staring ahead, her hardened, deliberative expression signalling nothing. *If the only option open to them was the one Babysitter had given them what would she do?* 'Maggie?'

'You can free me.' Maggie fixed Babysitter. 'Cut the rope.'

Babysitter didn't shift his scrutiny from Holly. 'Is that a joint decision?'

'Trust me, Holly.' Maggie turned her head slowly to her.

'What are you doing, Maggie?' Holly felt panic rise.

'Just trust me. Cut my rope.'

Had Maggie thought of a way out or was she willing to sacrifice anything to spend precious time with Penny?

Babysitter ambled over to Maggie.

'Wait!' Holly yelled.

'Your time is up. Maggie has volunteered.' Babysitter circled around Maggie and halted beside her. He held the scalpel up in front of her face.

Maggie's breath caught in her chest, the blade in his fingers at eye level.

'Perhaps I'll make this more interesting.' Babysitter considered the scalpel for a few seconds then slipped the handle into Maggie's right fist. 'Cut your own way out, Maggie.'

Maggie remained motionless.

Babysitter went to the trolley and picked up another scalpel. 'And you, Holly.'

He slid the cold handle into her palm.

When he stepped back Holly could see Maggie was already furiously sawing through the rope above her left wrist. Now she had no choice and started rapidly scoring hers.

'I think now is the time for me to wait outside. Whatever decision you come to—' Babysitter contorted and whirled around.

Haden was standing behind him, his bloodied left arm barely attached to his shoulder.

As he rounded on him Holly saw the two hypodermic needles stuck in Babysitter's back.

'You should've stayed down.' Babysitter picked up the axe from the trolley.

Holly could see that Haden could barely remain upright. Babysitter brought the blade down on him, and he crumpled with the first strike. He raised it again, and Haden screwed up his bloody face but Babysitter staggered back. 'Fuck.'

Whatever was in the hypodermics was working quickly into his system. He tottered forward and stepped on Haden's face to hold him down, but lost his balance and lumbered against the wall, striking it hard with his shoulder and dropping the axe.

Holly exchanged a look with Maggie. They'd both stopped to watch the struggle but knew that, whoever won, they were still in danger.

Their blades sawed vigorously.

Babysitter dropped to one knee, but then slid himself back up the wall.

Holly glanced up at her wrists. The blade had severed halfway through the rope. She returned her attention to the fight. Maggie's wrist was moving fast.

'You fucking...' Babysitter stumbled into the trolley, grabbed one of the bottles of liquid there and squirted it over Haden's prostrate form.

Haden did little to retaliate, and his eyes fluttered as he began to black out.

Babysitter doused Haden's torso and then leaned heavily on the trolley and selected the blowtorch from it.

Haden was conscious enough to see the flame and started to sob.

After clicking the ignition button twice the blowtorch ignited blue. Babysitter adjusted the flame so it was loose and yellow. He tried to stand, but seesawed on his heels before staggering back.

As he did Maggie was free. She thrust the scalpel into the side of Babysitter's neck.

CHAPTER SEVENTY-ONE

Maggie jerked her hand back as if she'd been electrocuted. It was exactly what she'd experienced when she'd planted the knife into Janet Braun. There had been nobody else in the bed with her. Janet hadn't woken. Her expression hadn't changed. Maggie had just stood and witnessed her ivory satin pyjamas turning red before she'd walked out of the room. It had been that quick. She'd gone into Daniel's nursery after. Held him for a few minutes then put him back in his crib. She'd done everything she was asked to do so she could spend her remaining time with Penny.

He wasn't going to take that away now.

Babysitter still had his back to her. The blowtorch slid out of his hand and dropped to the floor. The flame licked across the tiles, catching on a small pool of the flammable liquid he'd squirted over Haden. His fingers reached for the embedded scalpel.

But Maggie pulled it out and a jet of blood escaped. Babysitter's hand went instinctively to the wound, and he turned around, eyes rolling.

She could see Holly still hadn't freed herself.

Babysitter cast his gaze around and settled on the axe lying on the floor.

Maggie stepped forward with the scalpel. 'Touch it and I'll stick you again.' She'd killed before. He knew what she was capable of.

Babysitter tried to focus on her, and a half smile scuttled across his face.

A guttural scream broke the moment.

The flame had reached Haden and his whole body was on fire. He rolled onto his side, but it did nothing to smother the blaze.

Babysitter used the distraction to stumble away from Maggie towards Holly.

Maggie followed, dodging around the flames rising from Haden.

His hands were grabbing Holly's collar.

Maggie was on his back. 'Let her go!'

He squeezed Holly's throat. 'Stop her, Holly. I lied. I still have Abigail. Kill her.'

Holly's rope severed, and his bulk slammed her onto her spine.

Maggie took the piece of rope that was still tied around her right wrist, hooked it around his neck and jerked it back hard. 'I said let go of her!'

Babysitter choked. 'Kill her, Holly. Or you'll never see Abigail again.'

His weight was on Holly's arms, her hands either side of her face. She couldn't pull them out from underneath him to protect herself.

Maggie still had the scalpel. She released her grip on the rope, stabbed him in the neck again and felt his body jerk and his back rise as he tried to tug in a breath. She kept her body hugged hard to him.

Then she saw Holly reach into her sleeve with her left hand and pull something out. It looked like a pine cone.

Holly jammed it into his open mouth and pushed it hard to the back of his throat with her fingers. She screamed as he bit her, but pushed her hand further inside.

Maggie felt his body pump as he gagged and tried to wriggle free, but she held him there and jabbed the blade into him for the third time.

He retched and tried to wring Holly's neck, but his grip rapidly weakened.

They both held onto Babysitter until the toxins in his bloodstream had finished him. He stopped moving, but they didn't release him until they were sure he'd stopped breathing.

SEVENTY-TWO

As the Scion slogged back up the narrow lane, neither of them spoke. Even after racing through the forest to the car the smell of smoke was still on Holly. She wiped Babysitter's blood from her face but it felt like she was wearing a mask.

They'd escaped the icehouse and had found themselves in an underground storage room. Maggie had grabbed an old mattress there, dragged it into cold storage and dumped it on top of Haden to put out the fire, but it was already too late for him. Babysitter was motionless as well. There'd been no time to linger. They had to make sure Abigail and Penny were safe.

Maggie had her foot right down on the gas and, as they pushed on through the snow, Holly wondered if the engine would give out. She clenched her sticky fists tight in her lap as they headed back to the highway.

When she'd shoved the spiked flower head into Babysitter's mouth there was only one question in her mind. *Had he really taken Abigail home?* But she had no choice. He would have strangled her.

He'd said he'd been lying. Told her he still had Abigail. And now he was dead. *Had he been so sure of the decision Holly would make that he'd put her daughter back, or was she still being held in a location only he knew?*

'Sascha's place is on the way.'

Holly nodded once at Maggie. She must be terrified Babysitter might have been there. They had to check.

*

The journey was interminable. The snowfall intensified, as if it had redoubled its effort to frustrate their journey. As they approached Prospect Drive she scarcely registered the brilliant blue skies above them.

They pulled into Sascha's, Maggie got out of the car and left the engine running.

Holly slid into the driver's seat and watched her bang on the front door. She saw Sascha open it and an exchange. Sascha still had a bandage on her head, clutched her silver satin robe to her neck and looked perplexed but Maggie pushed her way inside, and they both disappeared. Holly held her breath. She had to wait. Make sure Penny was OK.

A few moments later Maggie reappeared clutching Penny in a blue blanket and made for the car.

Sascha was trailing behind her. 'Where the hell are you going now?'

'She's my child. I'll take her where I want.' There were tears of relief in Maggie's eyes.

Holly was happy for Maggie, but now she had to go.

Maggie reached the car. 'I'm coming with you.'

'You don't have to.' Holly looked back to reverse.

'Please, let me come.' She slid into the passenger seat with Penny.

Sascha had caught up. 'You must be insane to take her out into the cold like this.'

'I'll call you.' Maggie slammed the door. 'Let's go.'

Holly backed them out of the drive, and they took off.

Penny's sweet baby smell made the journey home excruciating, but she was glad that Maggie was with her.

Maggie kept quiet, her mouth gently kissing the top of Penny's head.

'This is it.' Holly pulled them sharply into her quiet suburban street.

'I'll go inside with you.'

Holly had the door open. 'No. Just tell me: what did he do when he returned Penny?'

'She was there when I got home. On the doorstep.'

Holly nodded and got out of the car. But there was no sign of Abigail outside the front door.

Panic choked her. *Was Abigail helpless and alone in a place far from here?*

She took her key from under the mat, unlocked the door and walked into the darkened and freezing lounge. *Had he really been in here?* Her hand shot to the light switch on the wall to her right and turned it on. She could see into her small kitchen. There was no sign somebody had forced their way in…

Dread was already swelling in her chest, and she moved quickly across the lounge rug to the stairs. She told herself to go straight up them, but still hesitated at the bottom. *What would she do if her daughter wasn't up there?*

Her feet started to climb, every step feeling heavier than the last until she was standing at the top, the early morning light dimly illuminating the indigo carpet between the closed doors. Abigail's sealed nursery was before her.

Kill her. Or you'll never see Abigail again.

Had Babysitter's last words to Holly been her last chance of saving her daughter?

Her gaze shot to the window at the end of the landing as something flitted past the pane. *A bird? The drone?*

She kept her eyes momentarily fixed on the powder blue sky.

Holly knew she couldn't delay the moment. She put her fingers on the cold handle of the stripped wooden door and turned it.

As the door cracked and Holly felt the cool draught from within, she could detect Abigail's unmistakable aroma. But the room always smelt like that.

Holly hovered at the threshold. The crib was positioned under the window, which was cracked open. Nothing looked to be out of place.

There were four paces between her and the crib. Then she'd be able to see inside. Holly felt her pulse quicken as she stepped into the room.

EPILOGUE

Holly negotiated her blue Mazda through the gap in the tall hedge and down the gravel track to the solitary bungalow on the plateau of grass below. Spring was trying to assert itself, and there were only a few patches of snow left. She'd already circled the location twice to make sure she wasn't being followed. The vacation property belonged to a friend of Sascha's and was just over sixty miles from Maggie's burnt-out Whitsun home.

She parked up, got out and looked back the way she'd come. It was the third time she'd visited but she still dreaded the idea she'd led the police there.

She opened the passenger door and took Abigail out of the baby seat. Her daughter hated being picked up now and was eager to walk everywhere, but today she was fast asleep so Holly carefully carried her to the bungalow.

Maggie was at the front door before she got there, and Holly could see how exhausted she was.

'Did she sleep all the way here?' Maggie whispered and ushered them both inside.

'Just dropped off.'

Penny was also sleeping in her crib by the picture window of the lounge, which overlooked the green valley below.

Maggie held out her arms for Abigail, and Holly passed her over.

'How's Penny's cough?'

Maggie gently bounced Abigail. 'Haven't had to give her Zyrtec since we got here. Maybe you were right about an allergy to something in the house.'

Holly nodded and left a gap for Maggie to fill, but she didn't.
'OK if I help myself to a coffee?' She headed to the kitchen.

Maggie followed. 'Let me. I've just made a fresh pot.'

'It's fine. Abigail loves it when you hold her.'

As Holly poured herself a cup she regarded the TV warbling in
the corner. It was the local morning news and, as usual, both of
them waited for Maggie's face to appear.

It had been nearly a month since Holly had found Abigail safe
in her crib. Babysitter had wrongly assumed that Maggie would
sacrifice herself, that the chain would be unbroken. But it hadn't
happened that way. After it was all over, Holly had warned Maggie
she couldn't delay telling the police the whole story and directing
them to the icehouse. Maggie had asked her to wait one hour before
she did and then drove away.

After they interviewed Holly, the police informed her that
Maggie and Penny had vanished.

A few days later, Sascha had visited Holly. She'd been questioned
by the police but insisted to them that she didn't know where her
sister and niece were, but she had lied. She revealed to Holly where
Maggie had gone and how to find her.

Maggie turned off the TV. 'I'm giving myself up tomorrow.'

Holly felt relief flood through her. 'You know it's for the
best.'

Maggie didn't meet her eye.

'Just tell the truth.' The truth was that Maggie had murdered
a stranger to save her child. But Holly had come so close to doing
that herself. *If she'd been in Maggie's shoes would she have done the
same?* 'I'll come in with you, give you support.'

'There's no need. You've told your side. It's time I told mine.'
She made her way back to the lounge.

Holly set her cup down and joined her. She watched Maggie
standing in the picture window, rocking Abigail and gazing down
at Penny as if it might be the last time. 'You should get the doctor

to check you out before you do.' It may have been a tiny shadow on her lung but it was cast long over what she'd done. *Was the threat of Maggie's own life being cut short what had made her mind up when she'd entered Janet Braun's home?*

'Penny spoke yesterday. Sounded like "Mamma".'

Holly guessed that was what Maggie had been waiting for. 'You knew she would. She was just doing it in her own time.'

'I can't get her to say it again.'

'She knows you're her mother.' Holly suspected Maggie had needed Penny's verbal acknowledgement of that though. 'And you're a good mother. How could you have put yourself through what you did if you weren't?'

Maggie patted Abigail.

Again, Holly wondered what Maggie had had in mind when she'd asked Babysitter to cut her ropes first. *What if Haden hadn't stepped in? Did Maggie have a plan? Or had she again been prepared to do whatever it took to enjoy these valuable moments with Penny?* Holly hadn't asked her and never would. 'You want me to have her back?' She held out her hands to take Abigail.

Maggie shook her head. 'It's fine.'

Holly dropped her arms.

'I'll go to the station this afternoon.'

Holly resisted the temptation to tell her again that she was doing the right thing. The police were looking for her, and Maggie was demanding too much of her and Sascha's loyalty. 'Please let me go with you.'

Maggie shook her head again. 'I'll be in touch.' She stared into the crib at Penny's imperturbable features. 'If it's not me that sees her first step can you make sure it's you?'

'I'll be there for Penny. And you know Sascha will be.' Holly knew what Maggie was thinking: how long did she have before her cancer stopped responding to treatment? And would she spend all of that time in police custody?

Holly went to stand beside her. 'It doesn't have to be this afternoon. Maybe leave it one more day.'

They both contemplated Penny's happily oblivious expression.

A LETTER FROM RICHARD PARKER

Thanks for buying *Keep Her Safe*. If you did enjoy it, and want to keep up-to-date with all my latest releases, just sign up at the following link. Your email address will never be shared and you can unsubscribe at any time.

www.bookouture.com/richard-parker

I hope it kept you turning or tapping the pages. Authors are nowhere without readers to breathe life into their characters and with the advent of so many entertainment platforms it's reassuring to see books still being consumed in paper or digital format. Imagination is king! I hope the next book you choose transports you somewhere strange and exciting.

If you've got time to rate this book or leave a brief review on Amazon that would really be great. It does make a huge difference. And please feel free to contact me on Twitter, Facebook or Instagram – readers saying hi can certainly lift a solitary writing day.

Richard Parker

groups/RichardJayParkerFans/

@Bookwalter

www.richardjayparker.com

ACKNOWLEDGEMENTS

There are a lot of books out there so I'm certainly grateful that you chose to read this one. Every reader brings their own imagination to a story and I wish I could see exactly what your Maggie and Holly look like! I really do appreciate you giving me your precious time and headspace. As always, kisses and eternal gratitude to my wife, Anne-Marie, who never complains when I get up in the early hours to spend time with psychopaths. I hope we don't make too much noise. A long and crushing cuddle to my Mum and Dad for supporting my writing for the last three decades. Love you both. Huge thanks to all the talented folk at Bookouture. Oliver Rhodes' crack team of friendly publishing professionals bring so much intelligence, enthusiasm and positive energy to every one of their books. Authors need incisive editors and I'm very lucky to have had Kathryn Taussig's experienced eye for this one. She has great instincts and the project has benefited enormously from them. I'd also like to particularly mention commercial manager, Natalie Butlin for her intuitive placement of my work, publicity and social media managers Kim Nash – I probably owe you a big gin with a slice of something exotic in it – and Noelle Holten who has an inspirational passion for books and all things criminal (within fiction, of course). Thanks also to Lisa Brewster at Black-sheep for the tenebrous and cool cover design, managing editor, Lauren Finger, copy editor Janette Currie, head of talent, Peta Nightingale, digital marketing manager, Alex Crowe, publishing assistant, Jennifer Hunt and much warmth to all the authors cluttering up the lounge. You're an exceptional bunch. Special salutes to Angie Marsons, Shalini Boland and Stephen Edger for their reviews. My work wouldn't see the light of day without the generosity and enthusiasm of committed bloggers who will happily promote authors on Twitter, Goodreads and Facebook for no other reason than they are passionate about the books they read. The importance of this can't be underestimated so heartfelt thanks to anyone who has given up their time to post a review or share them. These include Alison Drew, Magdalena Johansson, Renita D'Silva, Jen Lucas, Martha Cheeves, Joyce Juzwik, Nicki Richards, Amy Sullivan, Kelly Lacey, Sean Talbot, Rebecca Pugh, Claire Knight, Chelsea Humphrey, Ellie Smith, Lorraine Rugman, Steve Robb, Emma Welton, Stephanie Rothwell, Cleo Bannister, Abby Fairbrother, Donna Maguire, Sarah Hardy, Meggy Roussel, Sheila Howes, Karen Cole, Linda Strong, Maxine Groves, Joanne Robertson, Susan Hampson, Kate Moloney, Yvonne Mennink, Eva Merckx, Jules Mortimer, Norma Farrelly, Rachel Broughton, Kaisha Jayneh, Mandy White, Malina Skrobosinski, Shell Baker, Mandie Griffiths, Jo Ford, Kaz Lewis, Fran Hagan, Lisa Drewett, Carole Whiteley and Scott Griffin. Apologies to anyone I've missed. Get in touch and I promise to put you in the next one!

Made in the USA
San Bernardino, CA
19 March 2018